TWISTED
SANITY

TWISTED SANITY

MELINDA AVENT

TATE PUBLISHING
AND ENTERPRISES, LLC

Published by Tate Publishing & Enterprises, LLC
127 E. Trade Center Terrace | Mustang, Oklahoma 73064 USA
1.888.361.9473 | www.tatepublishing.com

Tate Publishing is committed to excellence in the publishing industry. The company reflects the philosophy established by the founders, based on Psalm 68:11,
"The Lord gave the word and great was the company of those who published it."

Published in the United States of America

ISBN: 978-1-63185-548-1
1. Fiction / African American / Contemporary Women
2. Fiction / General
15.01.26

Acknowledgement

Thank you to my family: Susie, JoAnn, Betty, and Keven. Your love and support was instrumental in the writing of this book. A special shout out to my very dear friend Joya whose friendship I will always cherish.

PROLOGUE

It was the summer of 1920 in Stump, Mississippi. A six-year-old black girl slowly walked down a dirt road. She was kicking small rocks and sticks as she walked along. A white boy of a similar age ran up to her and pulled on her plump braids. She yelled at him and pushed him away. He spat in her face and pushed her onto the ground.

"Dumb nigger," the boy shouted at the little girl.

Suddenly, a young black woman grabbed his arm and slapped him hard across his face two times. He fell to the ground holding his cheeks. The woman pointed her finger at him.

"Don't treat my daughter mean," the woman said angrily.

The boy cried as he scrambled to his feet and ran off. The little girl watched this scene wide-eyed as she wiped her sleeve across her cheek. The woman moved to hug the girl close.

"Why did he want to hurt me, Grandma?" asked the little girl.

"Sometimes, little boys do what they see their daddy do. It be wrong but ain't nobody to tell 'em that," Grandma Shay said angrily.

"I wish somebody would tell them it was wrong," the little girl sighed.

"Me too, Millie. Me too."

Keeping her arm around her granddaughter, they began walking down the long, dirt road.

CHAPTER 1

BROOKLYN, NY, 1972

Millie looked around the dining room table as her family gathered to eat the Sunday meal. Sunday supper had been a tradition in her southern black home for as long as she could remember. Having been raised by her grandmother, Millie remembered Grandma bustling around to prepare the Sunday meal. Even though they were poor, everyone could count on a grand Sunday dinner. There was plenty of food and lots of talking and laughing at the table. All of her aunts, sisters, and uncle would come to her grandmother's house for the delicious meal. It seemed the Shay family was made up of mostly women. The men either died or walked out on her aunts. Grandma only had one living brother, Uncle Hilliard. The family called him Hill. Grandma's three younger brothers, along with Millie's mother, had either died in freak accidents or of medical conditions that could have been treated had they not been living in Mississippi with no medical facilities that treated Negroes. Millie missed her mother, even though she was only eight months old when her mother died from pneumonia. She always imagined how it would have been had her mother lived. She just knew that having her mother with her would have made everything better. But regardless, she had her grandmother; to Grandma was all Millie needed. She revered her grandmother Molly. Grandma may have been strict but it had been for the best. She had wanted to grow up and be just like her. When Millie moved to Brooklyn, New York, she had continued the tradition in her own family. As a young child, she would help her grandmother set the table. She would beg to put the flatware at each place setting. Millie had felt so grownup as she laid out the forks and knives. It made her feel like she was part of the meal preparation. Looking at the varying faces of her family at the table helped her understand what it was to be a Shay.

"It sure is good to eat a home cooked meal," Jimmy said.

Sandra frowned as she looked at him.

"Are you saying I don't cook good meals?" Sandra said.

"Naw, baby! I'm not saying that at all," he replied quickly.

"Don't think that because I'm your wife I have to cook for you...because I don't," she said, hiding her smile as she looked down at her plate.

Jimmy didn't see her smile as he continued to explain himself.

"It's just that this smothered steak is so good. Not like those pork chops I had over at Robert's house the other night. Man, he offered me some chops and they almost took my teeth out!"

As everyone roared with laughter, Lisa wondered how Jimmy would get out of this. This was the reason that she loved having Sunday dinner with the family. It was full of jokes, laughter, and love.

"You didn't have to eat them," Josie objected. "And they weren't tough, just well done."

"An alligator would pass on those chops," Jimmy exclaimed.

"I've been cooking for years and those chops were tender and delicately simmered in a rich onion and mushroom sauce. I know how to cook! Tell him, Robert," Josie insisted.

Robert knew that as a loyal husband he should agree. But as an honest man...well, the truth was that those chops were hard as nails. It was a matter of deciding if he wanted to tell the truth and hear Josie's mouth for the rest of the night or tell a little white lie and have peace in his house. He decided to be honest and bear the pain.

"Well, maybe the chops needed to be tenderized a little more. They were a little on the tough side," he said bravely.

"What!" Josie yelled.

"Ha! His teeth screamed 'holy raw hide,'" Jimmy quipped.

"Hush!" Sandra punched her husband's arm.

"Mama! He doesn't appreciate me at all," Josie wailed.

"Yeah, I do. You just don't cook pork chops well—or steak or roast." Robert laughed.

"Well, you can eat at Sandra's place from now on," Josie yelled.

"Robert, you shouldn't be talking about your wife's cooking. She's a good cook," Millie said sternly.

"Just starve. See if I care!" Josie said as she got up and went into the kitchen.

Oh no, Lisa thought, Josie is really mad.

Robert hurriedly rose to follow Josie through the swinging kitchen door.

"Aw, baby! I was just kidding. Why you gotta be like that?" he complained.

Millie watched Robert enter the kitchen.

"Rob needs to show more understanding of his wife," Millie said sternly. "She cooks the best she can."

"He was just playing with her, Mama," Angela said. As the middle daughter, she was often the child to soothe her mother's ruffled feelings.

Lisa, the youngest daughter, piped up. "Besides, Josie's chops are tough," Lisa chuckled.

Everyone laughed except Millie. A young boy of nine years old said, "Mama, can we go outside?"

Sandra looked at him.

"Yes. All of you guys can go out and play," she said.

Three boys, ages six through ten, and a nine-year-old girl left the table and run through the kitchen to the back door. You could hear the back door bang close as they exited.

"Rob still shouldn't be talking about Josie. She's his wife. And you shouldn't either Jimmy. It ain't right. She cooks the best she can," Millie said.

"Jimmy and Robert were just teasing her. It ain't that serious, Mama," Sandra emphasized. She didn't feel that her words had the desired effect on her mother.

Lisa sighed. As usual, Mama couldn't take a joke. She saw Rob as being hurtful to Josie and wanted to stick her nose where it didn't belong.

Millie looked at them all severely as she rose and went through the swinging kitchen door. Everyone was quiet. Somehow the joy had left the room.

Josie was in the nursery putting her baby down for a nap. She tucked in the sleeping baby just as the phone rang. The baby woke and began crying loudly.

"Oh, damn!" Josie exclaimed.

She picked up her sobbing son and patted his back as she ran down the corridor to answer the phone on the hallway table. She quickly picked up the receiver.

"Hello. No. You have the wrong number."

She slammed the phone down in frustration. The baby continued to cry as she returned to the nursery and sat in a rocker. She began rocking and singing to the baby. Little Robbie fell asleep just as the door-bell rang.

"Nooo!" Josie moaned softly.

Josie rose to settle Robbie in the crib as the doorbell rang again. She tucked the blanket about the baby then ran down the corridor and the stairs to the front door. Opening the door, she said breathlessly, "Hi, Mama."

Millie entered the brownstone carrying a casserole bowl. "Are you all right?" Millie asked in concern.

Josie closed the door. "Yes. I just ran from upstairs to answer the door," Josie said. "I'd just gotten little Robbie down for a nap and I didn't want the bell to wake him."

"Oh, I'm sorry. I didn't mean to wake him," Millie apologized.

"You didn't. He's still asleep," Josie said. "What do you have there?"

"I made this chicken casserole for you. I thought you could use a night off from cooking," Millie explained.

"Oh, Mama, thank you! But you didn't have to do that," Josie smiled.

Millie took her coat off and hung it on the coat rack. "I know I didn't have to. I wanted to," Millie said. "With the new baby and all, I know you don't have time to think straight, let alone do a lot of cooking."

"That's for sure. But Robbie's sleeping now so I have a moment to rest," Josie sighed.

They moved through the common rooms to the kitchen. Josie put the casserole in the refrigerator and turned on the kettle to heat some water.

"You want some tea, Mama?" she asked.

Millie sat down at the round table. "Yes, I think I do," Millie replied.

Josie put the kettle on to boil then moved to take two mugs from the cupboard. After putting tea bags in the mugs, she moved to the table and set the mugs down. She took a seat expelling a heavy sigh. "Oh! It's good to sit for few minutes," Josie said as she slumped into the chair. "I've been on the go all day. Taking care of a newborn, a nine-year-old, and doing housework is no joke!"

"Nobody said it would be easy. I wondered why you insisted on having a baby. But you were determined to give that man a child."

Josie took a deep breath. "Rob and I wanted to have a child." Josie slowly exhaled. "There's nothing wrong in starting a family. We're building our lives together."

"You already have Kimberly. There was no rush to have a baby," Millie said stubbornly.

"Rob loves Kimberly as if she were his own. But I wanted to give him a child that was his. I wanted to give my husband that gift." Josie was almost pleading for her mother's understanding. She didn't want to continue to have this conversation with her. She wanted her mother to accept Rob and this child and know that she was happy in her family. She didn't understand why her mother was fighting so hard against it.

"Another baby could have waited. You're still young. You have plenty of time. Robert should love Kimberly like she's his own and be satisfied," Millie reasoned.

"He does, Mama. He loved Kimberly the moment he met her. I could not have hoped for more. But he wanted us to have a child together. And I wanted that too," Josie explained patiently.

The kettle whistled and Josie began to rise. Millie rose quickly.

"You sit there and rest. I'll pour the tea," Millie said.

Josie hoped her mother would accept her explanation and not start in on Rob. She just wasn't up to it today. Her mother had never been keen on Robert from the beginning of her relationship with him. She never understood why but Millie took an instant dislike to the man and there's been nothing he could do to change her feelings. She had hoped that her marriage to him and the family's favorable attitude toward Rob would change Millie's mind about him. But it hadn't. At times, she thought that Millie's ill feelings toward him had intensified. She was at her wits end in figuring out how to rectify the matter. Rob tried to win Millie over but she wouldn't budge in her viewpoint. She was afraid that Rob would soon tire and stop trying.

Millie went to the stove to get the kettle and returned to pour the hot water into the mugs. Returning the kettle to the stove, she moved back to the table and sat down.

"Does Rob help out around the house?" Millie asked.

"Not much. I have to get on him to do the least little thing," Josie said without thinking. She stirred sugar into her tea. "Lately, my requests have triggered an argument. So to avoid arguing with him, I just don't ask him to do anything. I wish he would do more, especially now that we have little Robbie."

"He won't help you with the baby? What kind of daddy is that?" Millie exclaimed in shock.

Josie quickly tried to correct her error in saying anything. "Rob is a wonderful dad," Josie emphasized. "He loves little Robbie to death. He plays with him all the time. He just isn't big on changing diapers. I guess that's a man for you." Josie chuckled, trying to ease the tension.

Millie did not laugh. She looked at Josie and wondered why she put up with all of Rob's faults. She certainly wouldn't.

"Robert isn't doing his part. You shouldn't have to do it all," Millie said sternly.

"Don't start, Mama. Rob works hard at the factory. I know he's very tired when he gets home," Josie objected.

"You work hard at the salon. You're on your feet all day dealing with those hoity-toity women that's never satisfied," Millie snorted.

"The women aren't that bad, Mama," Josie smiled. "Most of them are my friends."

Millie blew air into her cup to cool the tea. "My point is that you work just as hard on your job as Robert and you still take care of the kids. He needs to do the same," Millie said.

"Well, right now, I'm on maternity leave, so he figures I can handle it," Josie replied.

"He figures wrong. And I'm going to tell him so when he gets home," Millie snapped.

"No, you're not. I don't want you arguing with Rob. I can deal with my husband," Josie said in alarm. She didn't want her mother interfering.

"Will he help out with the kids?" Millie was suspicious.

"Yes," Josie said, hoping her answer would satisfy Millie.

Millie did not believe her. "No, he won't. He probably won't even be here tonight," Millie retorted.

Josie was surprised at Millie's comment. "Why would you think that?"

"It's Wednesday night, ain't it? His night to be out with the boys?" Millie said knowingly.

"I guess. But he may not even go. Anyway, how do you know?" Josie asked.

"I know a lot of things. He's going to take off and not give two thoughts about you. As if you don't need a night out with the girls! Oh, that man needs talking to!" Millie was angry.

Josie looked Millie in the eye. She wasn't sure why Millie was so heated but she had to set her straight.

"But not by you, Mama! It's not your business," Josie said firmly.

"Then you should have kept your business to yourself," Millie retorted.

"I tried," Josie muttered to herself.

Millie stood and walked briskly down the hall to the to the coat rack. She hurriedly put her coat on. Josie followed quickly.

"Mama, don't say anything to Rob. Stay out of it!" Josie pleaded.

Millie gave Josie a hard, no-nonsense look.

"Straighten that man out, girl. If you don't, I will!" Millie warned.

Millie opened the door and left. She swiftly stumped down the walkway to the sidewalk. Turning to her left, she continued her journey never looking back at Josie. Not a nod or a wave of her hand. Nothing. No goodbyes or hugs from Millie. Josie closed the door and leaned against it. She should be used to her Mama's cold ways by now. Millie was a hard woman.

Josie tried to hold the door of the diner open and push her stroller into the restaurant but the door refused to stay open long enough for her to accomplish the task. Just as frustration was getting the best of her, a gentleman held the door open for her.

"Entry awaits," he smiled.

When Josie smiled her gratitude to him, he caught his breath. He was astounded at her beauty.

She's gorgeous, he thought.

"Thanks again." Josie waved at the man as she pushed the stroller to the coffee counter. She was completely unaware that he was staring at her through the door.

Sandra was wiping down the counter but glanced up in time to witness the incident at the door. She saw the man's reaction to Josie's beauty. Everyone who knew Josie knew that she was incredibly beautiful—everyone except Josie. Her smile transformed her face into graceful loveliness that held you spellbound. It took you a while to get accustomed to it. But Josie was totally oblivious to her beauty. She just went about her way completely ignorant of the impact she had on people. Her looks gave her a tremendous power that most women would kill for. She could have anything or anyone she wanted with a simple beckon of her finger, little did she know. That is what made her so special. Having had a baby recently had not applied excessive pounds to her 5'3" frame. She was still slender and lithe. Her lovely hazel eyes were warm and kind and her smooth brown skin held an earthy glow that nearly all post-pregnant women envied. She smiled and shook her head as Josie blithely approached the counter. Josie saw Sandra shake her head.

"Hi Sandy! What's wrong?" Josie asked innocently.

Sandra came around the counter and hugged Josie. "Oh, nothing," Sandra answered. "What brings you here on such a gloomy day? I don't think the sun is going to show its face today."

Sandra bent to tickle little Robbie in the stroller. He gurgled his pleasure. Sandra chuckled.

"I just needed to get out of the house," Josie sighed. "The walls were inching in on me."

"Come on," Sandra urged. "Let's sit."

They moved to a booth and sat down. Josie maneuvered the stroller beside her. Robbie soon fell asleep. Eric, the waiter, came over. "Can I get you anything?" he asked.

"Two iced teas would be good," Sandra said.

"Sure thing," Eric replied as he retreated to the kitchen.

"Now, what caused the walls to close in on you?" Sandra asked.

"You know me so well," Josie murmured.

"I'm your sister. I know you like I know myself. What's bothering you?" Sandra stated simply.

"In a word, Mama," Josie said emphatically.

"Oh God! What now?" Sandra asked. She wasn't sure if she really wanted to know the answer. Her mother was forever sticking her nose where it didn't belong. And the situation always came to a bad end when she did. Her mother would never learn to let things be and they would resolve themselves.

"As usual, she thinks she needs to fix something but it really doesn't need her hand in it at all," Josie exclaimed.

"What does she think she needs to fix?" Sandra asked.

Suddenly, Josie was hesitant. She wanted to unload to Sandra but she didn't want her to know just how much of a jerk Robert was being.

"Well…" Sandra prompted.

"Rob," Josie responded reluctantly.

"Rob?" Sandra was confused. Was there something going on with them that she didn't know about? She thought all was well between them. Jimmy had mentioned Rob's harsh attitude toward Josie the night he had the infamous chops at Josie's house. Sandra had chalked it up to Rob having a hard day at work then coming home to a badly cooked meal. Any man would be miffed.

"What about Rob?" Sandra prompted.

"She wants to tell Rob off about not helping me more around the house. She thinks he's not doing his part," Josie poured out.

"More like curse him out. And how is it that she thinks Rob doesn't help you?" Sandra questioned. She had a sneaky suspicion that Josie had been talking too much.

Eric arrived with their drinks.

"Thanks, Eric," Sandra said.

"You bet," Eric replied as he walked away.

Josie sat quietly.

"Well? Spill it, Josie. Why does Mama think that way?" Sandra insisted.

"I…well…perhaps I mentioned a word or two about him being lazy," Josie said sheepishly.

"Josie!" Sandra exclaimed.

"It was out before I knew it. I didn't really mean it," Josie explained.

"You know how Mama is," Sandra said in shock. "She will twist that information around and have people thinking that Rob's the worst criminal alive."

"I know," Josie moaned. "I didn't mean to say anything. I was just so tired and frustrated and I said it without thinking."

Sandra took pity on her and reached across the table to hold her hand. She empathized.

"Honey, I know you didn't mean to say as much as you did but Mama only requires an inch and she'll take way more liberty than she should."

"I guess I wasn't thinking until it was too late," Josie said miserably. "I can't take the words back. And even if I could, Mama wouldn't forget them. I'm so afraid she's going to say something to Rob and it erupts into a huge argument. And all of my hard work in coaxing them to get along would be blown to bits!"

"I know you been working on Mama to like Rob more. I don't understand why she doesn't. Let's just hope that she doesn't say anything to him. Hopefully, she won't see him any time soon and when she does, she will have cooled off. Maybe you should tell Rob that Mama may say something to him," Sandra reasoned.

"I can't! He'll be furious!" Josie was appalled.

"But he'll be forewarned." Sandra pulled her hand back to her side of the table and continued. "I can't believe you told Mama something like this. You know how she can be."

Josie pouted as she said, "It was a slip. You've told Mama stuff that you later wished you hadn't."

Sandra took a deep breath. Josie was right. She wish she could take back some of the things she had confided to her mother. Mama had a knack of bringing the subject up when she knew you didn't want to talk about it. And she always wore a smug smile while watching you squirm. It was a subtle dig that she perversely enjoyed. She knew how Josie would feel if she didn't tell Rob and Mama opened her mouth. She was in a no-win situation.

"Yeah, you're right," Sandra said as she reigned in her thoughts. "We all have talked when we shouldn't. But believe me, Rob may be mad when you tell him but you'll be much better off if you do. Enduring Rob's anger now is much better than suffering Mama's control later on," Sandra counseled.

"You're right. I'll tell Rob. Just have your spare room available in case Rob's fury is more than I can take," Josie said miserably.

Sandra chuckled. "It will be all right," she said.

Josie took a deep swallow of her iced tea and asked. "So tell me," Josie began, "what do you want me to do for Mama's birthday party next week?"

"Well, Angie has sent out invitations. Lisa's band is going to play. The diner is cooking the food…" Sandra trailed off.

"What about decorations? I can decorate the place," Josie said as she looked around the diner in thought. She started taking mental notes of what she would like to do.

"Perfect! You're so good at that kind of thing." Sandra was delighted. She could cook barbecue but ribbons, balloons, and such was not her thing.

"I'm glad we're doing this," Josie said. "Mama isn't all bad."

"No. She has some really awesome qualities. She's a very good person most of the time," Sandra mused.

"Yeah, she is," Josie agreed.

They continued talking for some time until Josie realized she needed to get home. She grabbed her baby bag and hurriedly pushed the stroller out of the diner. Sandra sat there thinking about Josie's coming conversation with Rob. She did not want to be in Josie's shoes.

"Hi, Mama," Sandra greeted her mother as she stepped out onto the back stoop.

Millie was on her knees working in her vegetable garden as usual. Millie looked up. "Hi, Sandra. Shouldn't you be at the diner?" Millie asked.

"I'm on my way but I wanted to drop off a cherry pie for you," Sandra grinned.

"Mmm, now you know I love some cherry pie. Thank you," Millie said appreciatively.

"You're welcome. You're always doing something kind for one of your kids, I wanted to do something nice for you," Sandra smiled.

"Well, you know there isn't anything I wouldn't do for my girls. Accept I ain't going to prison for you. You're on your own with that." Millie laughed.

Sandra laughed too. "I know, Mama. You've told us often enough." She chuckled. "But there is another reason I wanted to stop by."

"What's that?" Millie peered at her.

"Your birthday is coming up and we're going to throw you a party," Sandra said. "I'm letting you know now. We all know you don't like surprises."

"Sandra, I told you all I didn't want a party," Millie complained.

"Mama, you say that every year but you have more fun at the party than any one there," Sandra countered.

"Well, I don't want it," Millie said stubbornly.

"Well, you're getting it. So get used to the idea," Sandra said flatly.

"Humph!"

Sandra laughed. "Mama, you will dance us all under the floor." She grinned. "I got to go. See you later." Sandra waved as she entered the house to leave. Millie slowly smiled as she began to dig in the dirt.

CHAPTER 2

Millie stared out the window. *What a gloomy day,* she thought. *It looks like it will rain before long. And I promised Gladys I would bring by a pot of vegetable soup.* Gladys wasn't doing well after her hip surgery and Millie wanted to help out all she could.

Millie wandered back to the couch and plopped down. She spied the photo album on the coffee table. She leaned forward to pick it up then settled back against the sofa. She sees an old black and white picture of her mother. It was the only thing she had that told her anything about her mama. Maime Lee Shay had died when Millie was eight months old. Grandmama Molly had said that her mother, Maime got a cough and it never went away. The cough just got worse and worse. Negroes couldn't get any kind of medicine in those days. The doctors wouldn't make house calls to them and the hospital for Negroes was a hundred miles away. One night, she was coughing up blood as thick as molasses. Grandmama said she thought the blood would strangle her, it was so thick. She got so weak but she managed to beg her mother to take care of her daughters Millie and

Bethelee. She knew that she wouldn't make it through the night. Deep into the night, Maime gave her last cough. She just couldn't hold on to life any longer. She was dead. This photograph was all that Millie had of her mother. Millie always wondered if her life would have been any different had Maime lived. She would never know but she had to be grateful that she did have her grandmother to raise her. Grandmama brought her up well even if Millie didn't always understand her reasons for doing things. Grandmama always knew best. A motto Millie never doubted. Flipping the pages, she chuckled at some of the pictures until she saw one from years ago. The picture was in black and white and was old and worn. Millie ran her large, strong fingers over the photo. It reflected a young black man standing in front of a small, dilapidated house. Standing next to him was a young Millie with a baby in her arms and a toddler at her side. Millie looked closely at the picture and recalled the events of that day.

Millie was in the tiny kitchen washing dishes. She heard commotion at the back door and looked around as Ray "String Bean" Hawkins came in smiling from ear to ear. She smiled at him and asked, "What you up to, String Bean?"

Everybody called Ray "String Bean" for the obvious reason. He was skinnier than a splinter cut in two. String Bean had long since grown used to the nickname and actually liked it. He grinned, showing a missing front tooth, but that didn't stop him from smiling widely as he showed off his new camera. He said, "Looka here! I gots me a brand new camera. Where's Leon? I wanna

MELINDA AVENT

take a picture of ya'll and the younguns." He extended the camera to her.

Millie wiped her hands on her dingy apron and held the camera carefully. "This sure is pretty. How you afford it?" she asked.

"I's got some extra money for cleaning out old man Tucker's back shed. There was more junk in it than flies buzzin' round collard greens on a hot day! But the money he gives me bought me this here camera. So's I guess it was worth it," String Bean said proudly.

"Sure is nice, String Bean. That it is." Millie admired it.

As Millie continued looking at it, her husband, Leon, came in the house from the front porch. He was a tall, well-built black man with a small goatee. All the women thought he was a fine looking man. He thought so too.

"I thought I heard talking," Leon said.

Millie showed the camera to Leon and said, "String Bean got himself a brand new camera."

Leon took the camera from Millie and said, "Well, this is real nice. Let's us go out and take some pictures. Come on Millie. Get the kids."

Millie quickly took off the apron and picked up baby Sandra from the crib. She called to the toddler who was on the sitting room floor playing with a rag doll. "Come on, Josie. Come with Mama."

The toddler stood up on shaky legs and moved to Millie. She hurried out the back door. She didn't want to keep Leon waiting. He was in a good mood and she wanted him to stay that way. She took Josie's hand and went outside. Leon and String Bean did a lot of laughing and talking while they were taking pictures. After String Bean took their picture, he left saying he had more stops to make. Leon came into the house.

"Where's my dinner, woman?" Leon said sharply.

Millie put Sandra back in the crib and led Josie into the sitting room to play with her doll. She then entered the kitchen and looked at Leon's angry face. The pot roast still had another fifteen minutes to cook. Leon would not be happy.

"The pot roast ain't quite ready. It needs about fifteen more minutes," Millie said quietly.

"You know what time I likes to eat. Why didn't you cook it sooner?" he yelled. He threw his arm back and slapped her hard across the face.

Millie stumbled backward and clutched her face and stared at him in fear and anger. She refused to cry though. He would not see her shed a tear for the likes of him.

"Well? What you got to say for yourself? You gonna give me some pitiful excuse as to why you can't cook a simple meal on time," he taunted her.

She refused to answer him. He wouldn't accept her answer anyway. He raised his arm and hit her again. Millie fell against the table.

"I'll go down to the joint and git me some good food," he said scornfully. "I'll git me some good company too." He smirked as he left the house. The screen door banged shut eerily. She righted herself and cupped the side of her face. The pain was almost unbearable. Soon she heard the old Ford truck rattle down the dirt road.

Millie went into the sitting room and looked at Josie. Josie looked up at her with big tears in her eyes. Millie picked up the child and sat down in the old wooden rocking chair. She took a handkerchief from her pocket and wiped away Josie's tears, then snuggled the child against her ample bosom and began rocking. She hummed a tuneless melody as she thought about when Leon would stumble back home in a drunken state. The rocking motion soon put Josie asleep. Millie continued to hum and rock.

The memory began to fade. Millie sighed. It was over and Leon was gone. She closed the photo album just as Lisa entered the house. Lisa glanced into the living room and saw Millie sitting on the sofa.

"Hi, Mama. What are you doing?" Lisa said.

Millie put the photo album back on the low cocktail table. "Nothing." Her tone was sharp.

Lisa heard the abrupt tone in Millie's voice and wondered what's wrong with her. She had seen Millie return the album to the table. She wondered if it had something to do with her mother's bad mood. Lisa sat down next to Millie and reached for the photo album. She opened it and began looking at the photos. Millie sat silent and stiff. Lisa pointed out the picture Millie had been looking at.

"Look at this one, Mama. That's daddy and you with Josie and Sandra," Lisa said. "Sandra was just a baby."

"Yes," Millie said, tight-lipped.

"It's a good picture of the four of you. Daddy looks happy but you aren't smiling. Why weren't you smiling, Mama?" Lisa asked innocently.

Millie did not feel like talking, especially about that picture. "I don't know. I didn't feel like it I guess," Millie said shortly.

"Oh! Look at this one, Mama!" Lisa exclaimed when she turned the next page.

Millie looked at the picture but said nothing.

"It's daddy standing next to his old Ford truck. What was he like, Mama? You've never told me anything about him," Lisa asked.

"I've told you about him," Millie said.

"No, you haven't," Lisa returned.

"Well, maybe because there's nothing much to tell," Millie said flatly.

Lisa decided not to push Millie for information about her father. She guessed her mother would open up in her own time. But at the rate she's going, that might be never. Lisa remembered asking her mother about her father when she was about seven years old and Millie had said that Leon was "dead and gone" and nothing else. That piece of data told Lisa precious little about her father. Lisa was nineteen years old now and her mother had remained silent on the subject. She was beginning to think that she would never learn anything more about her daddy. Lisa looked at another photo.

"Here's Richard and Patrick," Lisa said. "It's hard to believe that they're gone."

"It's been seven years since they passed," Millie said quietly.

"It was so odd how they died such a short time apart from one another. There wasn't six months between their deaths. To this day, the police have not found the person who stabbed them. I guess they never will. I still miss them," Lisa sighed.

Millie stood up and moved toward the kitchen. "I'm not going down memory lane," Millie said sharply. "I made chicken and dumplings, do you want any?"

Lisa was surprised at Millie's curt tone. Her mother didn't want to continue the conversation so she tersely put an end to it. She stood there looking like a commanding officer with zero tolerance. Lisa wondered what was going through Millie's mind at that moment. Lisa decided she needed time away from her.

"No. I'll eat later," Lisa responded.

Millie turned and walked away. Lisa watched her retreating back until she went through the kitchen swinging door.

Millie's birthday party were in full swing. Lisa finished her song and took her bow. She waved to the crowd amidst cheers and applause, then left the stage. In her excitement, she practically skipped to her mother's table. She hugged Millie.

"See, Mama. I told you my band was really good. And we are going to make it big. No doubt about it. Our manager said a recording contract is in the bag!" Lisa said excitedly.

"Maybe so," Millie said doubtfully.

"Gee, thanks," Lisa feigned happiness.

Millie did not comment.

Lisa shook her head and went back to the stage as Derek sat down at the table. "Hey Mama, are you having a good time?" her son-in-law asked.

"Yes, I am. You children shouldn't have gone to all this trouble," she smiled.

"It was no trouble. You don't turn fifty-eight every day." He grinned.

"Thank you for reminding me," she said dryly. "I had forgotten my age."

He laughed. "You don't look a day over forty."

"Liar!"

"God's truth. Mrs. Barnes would kill to look as good as you," Derek smiled.

"She probably would but she won't be getting any beauty tips from me," Millie said slyly.

Derek shook his head. "You're not right, mama," he grimaced.

"But it's fun." She laughed. "You know, the girls didn't have to do all this. I'm happy with just my daughters around me. I don't need all this." She gestured to the room full of people.

"You know your daughters would never let your birthday pass without celebrating it," he said. "Besides, I think the entire neighborhood looks forward to your birthday parties. It's the event of the year."

"I think the entire neighborhood and a few extras showed up. I don't know half of these people," Millie complained.

"Don't worry, Mama. I'll take care of any crashers." He puffed up his chest. "I'm a cop after all. I get to flash my badge and be the man."

Millie laughed. "Ooh! I'm scared of you!" she exclaimed. She then took his hand. "You're a good man, Derek. I'm real glad my Angela has you for a husband."

He grinned. "I'm real glad your Angela would have me. I really love her, you know," he said soberly.

"I know you do. The two of you have always belonged together. I just wish Robert was more like you," Millie said brusquely. "Josie deserves someone like you."

"Rob is a good man. He loves Josie very much," Derek said. He didn't like the path this conversation was taking.

"He doesn't act like it. Not like you." Millie was disbelieving.

Derek chuckled. "He's not me, Mama. Rob is his own man and he shows his love for Josie in his own way. But make no mistake, he's in love with his wife."

"How do you know?" she asked doubtfully.

"Because he told me so," Derek said simply. "And I believe him. There's nothing in this world that he wouldn't do for his family. That's how much he loves them."

Millie harrumphed. "I won't have him treating my daughter mean. I won't stand for it," she said adamantly.

"He loves her, Mama," he reiterated. "He's not going to treat her badly." Derek was a little perturbed at Millie's vehemence. He looked closely at her. She was a large-boned, tall woman whose temperament was far from mild. She could be cantankerous and rude when dealing with someone she didn't like. Her stature and build made her a daunting and intimidating figure. She could be a fearsome and intimidating woman when angered. But he had seen the softer side of Millie as well. She had always treated him with warmth, fondness, and respect. She could be kind, caring, loving, and funny when she wanted to be. She had just as many friends who loved her as she had enemies who detested her. Millie was a very private and complex woman, a tough puzzle to assemble.

"He treats her like crap and it needs to stop," Millie snapped.

"Don't worry about them, Mama. They may have some ups and downs but they will work it out," he said hoping to calm her.

"So you say," Millie said, unconvinced.

Derek smiled as he stood. "Yes, I do," he said.

"He had better fix his ways or I…"

"Or you'll what, Mama?" Derek was a little worried about Millie's attitude.

"Nothing." She wouldn't say anything more.

"It's going to be okay. You'll see," Derek tried to ease her concern.

"We'll see." That was all Millie was willing to concede.

"They're playing Angie's favorite song," Derek said, trying to sound casual.

"Then you'd better go dance with her." Millie smiled.

"Just what I plan to do," he answered. He leaned over and kissed Millie's cheek and said, "Happy birthday, Mama."

He walked over to Angela's side and pulled her onto the dance floor. Millie watched them for a moment then her gaze travelled to Robert who was talking and laughing with some men. Millie compared him to Derek and he came up very short. Too short for comfort.

～

"You remembered," Angela turned up her glowing face to her husband.

"No way could I forget our wedding song. I was the lucky man who got the bride. I'll never forget holding you in my arms, dancing until the wee hours of the morning," Derek smiled down into her lovely face.

"Everyone should feel the way I do. You make me so very happy, Derek." Angela sighed as she laid her head on his chest.

He pulled her close, encircling her waist. He was one blessed man and he would never take it for granted. Angela was a gift from God and he would be eternally grateful. He just wished Millie could see that Josie and Robert had the same kind of chemistry, just different from what she expected.

"Hey! Where are you? You seem a million light years away?" Angie asked.

He looked down at her and said, "Just thinking. Mama is having a hard time seeing Josie and Robert's marriage as a loving relationship. She's pretty hard on Robert."

"Well, there are times when Robert could be a little more understanding. Josie has a lot on her. It's hard having to do it all," Angie said.

"Rob has a lot on him too. He's a man that knows his responsibilities. It's difficult for him to admit that he may need help," Derek said softly.

Angie stopped dancing and said in alarm. "Are they in financial trouble?"

"I think so. Rob told me that he may need to get a second job. It's hard for a man to feel that he can't provide for his family," Derek surmised.

"We can help, can't we?" Angela asked worriedly.

"Yes. But getting Rob to accept it is another story."

"Men and their pride!" Angie scoffed.

"Baby, sometimes pride is all a man has," he explained.

"But it doesn't put food on the table," she said flatly.

"Maybe not. But it makes a man feel like King Kong when he doesn't have to swallow it," he stated. "Let's give it some more time and see how things turn out."

The music stopped and Derek and Angie turned to applaud the band. The band was striking up another tune. A woman approached Derek and solicited a dance from him.

"All slow dances belong to his wife," Angela said kindly.

She shrugged and walked away. Derek smiled down at Angie as he pulled her close and slowly swayed to the music.

Lisa looked out into the crowd from the stage and saw her mother dancing up a storm. She smiled wanly. She wished her mother could be happy like that all the time. But something haunted her. It made her obsessively protective of her daughters. Her Mama often went to the extreme in trying to shelter them. She wondered at times how far her mother would go to shield her girls from what she thought was bad.

Angela, Derek, Sandra, and Jimmy all joined Josie at her table. They were exhausted. Jimmy looked out on to the floor and spotted Millie dancing. He exclaimed, "Look! Mama is dancing with old Mister Cook."

"She's loving it. Her face is lit up like a Christmas tree!" Angela grins.

"Girl, they're doing the Jitter Bug!" Sandra laughed.

"Mama's got some moves. Ladies, take notes," Derek joked.

"I'm glad she's having a good time," Josie said.

Robert joined the group. Josie refused to look at him. He hadn't helped her at all with the baby. He'd been missing in action all night. At one point, he even left the premises. Where did he go? And with whom? She was furious with him and she was letting him know it.

"So am I. It's her day after all. She should enjoy it," Robert said.

"Where have you been?" Josie's golden brown eyes were blazing.

"I had some business to take care of," he said evasively.

"In the middle of Mama's party?" Josie was flabbergasted.

He took little Robbie from her. "I'll keep him for the rest of the night."

Josie was astounded. She couldn't believe her ears. Robert looked a little sheepish as he held the baby. Josie's anger instantly melted; although she still wondered about his activities.

"Come on, Josie. You haven't danced all night," Jimmy said as he grabbed Josie's hand and pulled her onto the dance floor. They joined a line dance. Sandra joined the dance as well.

Derek decided to lean over and kissed Angela just as Lisa approached the table.

"Sorry to interrupt."

"Yeah, I bet you are," Angela laughed good-naturedly.

Lisa grinned as she took a seat. "I wanted to ask Derek something," Lisa said.

"What's up, Brat?" Derek teased her.

Lisa frowned at his use of his nickname for her. He had started calling her that name the first day he'd met her and he hadn't stopped. Everyone had thought it was cute and the name stuck. She could have happily strangled him for it. But getting him to stop using the name now was a lost cause so she just tried to ignore it.

"How come the police never caught the person who killed Patrick and Richard?" Lisa asked.

"Lisa! Why do you ask now?" Angela was perturbed.

"Why not now? The crime has never been solved," Lisa said.

"Any other time would be better than at Mama's birthday party," Angela snapped.

"The police didn't have any clues to work with," Derek answered seriously. "It happened before I transferred into this precinct. But from what I heard, the detectives had zilch to go on."

"Hmm," Lisa pondered.

"Why the sudden interest?" Derek probed.

"It's not really sudden. I've always wondered why the case was unsolved. I saw their pictures in a photo album a few days ago and it got me to thinking. They were both killed by the same knife, right? Doesn't that mean that the same person murdered them?" Lisa surmised.

"It stands to reason. But without the knife and lack of additional evidence, the police had nothing that would lead them to the murderer," Derek explained.

"Man! I wish we could find that knife. It would solve the case. But I guess it's too late now. That knife is probably long gone," Lisa replied somberly.

Angela and Derek looked at each other, both wondering why Lisa was so intent on this now. It was puzzling.

Jimmy and Josie came back to the table.

"It looks like the party is winding down," Josie said. "We'd better start cleaning up."

Josie turned to move toward the cluttered tables. She pulled Jimmy along to help. Lisa and Angela followed. Derek sat quietly, thinking about what Lisa had said.

Derek sat in bed watching Angela slip into her night-gown. As she brought her head through the opening of the neckline, she said. "I wonder why Lisa questioned Richard and Patrick's death now?"

"She said seeing their photos triggered the memory of their deaths. I guess it just doesn't sit well with her. I remember you saying that she was very close to Patrick and Richard," he said.

Angela climbed into bed and fluffed her pillow. She sat back against them. "Yeah! She was crazy about them," she responded. "They were the brothers she never had. That's not to say that she doesn't love you, Derek, and Jimmy as well, but Richard and Patrick—" she trailed off.

"Richard and Patrick were first. They had a special bond. It's okay. I understand. She was pretty young when it happened, wasn't she?" Derek asked.

"She was about twelve," Angela answered.

"Too young for her opinions to matter to anyone. Now that she's older, maybe she wants to see if she can help solve the mystery," he said.

He pulled Angela close to him as she said, "Derek."

"Hmm."

"Do you think you could go over the case files of Patrick and Richie?" she asked.

"Aww! Angie! I'm sure the—"

"Just to make sure the detectives didn't miss anything. Please, honey! For Lisa? For me?" she pleaded.

He rolled on top of her and looked down at her. "There's not much I would deny Lisa. And there's absolutely nothing I wouldn't do for you. I'll pull the files and look them over."

She smiled and gave him a peck on the mouth. "Thank you, honey!" She smiled.

"Oh, you'll have to do better than that."

He lowered his head and kissed her deeply.

CHAPTER 3

Lisa happily bounded down the steps the next evening. She saw Millie in the parlor sitting in her rocker.

"Mama, I'm leaving. I have a gig at the club tonight," Lisa said brightly.

"How long are you going to continue messin' around at that honk-a-tonk? When are you going to get a real job?" Millie snorted.

The joy left Lisa's spirit. "Mama, I thought you were okay with me singing with my band. You saw me perform at your birthday party and you seemed fine with it," Lisa reasoned.

"I wasn't going to make a fuss about it at the party. But I don't like you on that stage flaunting yourself," Millie said harshly.

"I'm not flaunting, I'm singing and dancing. It's called entertaining the audience. And I'm damned good at it," Lisa snapped.

"Watch your mouth, girl. You may talk that way at that joint but not with me," Millie ripped at her.

"I'm not having this conversation with you," Lisa retorted as she snatched her jacket off of the coat rack.

"You had better quit your singin'," Millie stated.

"Or what?" Lisa challenged.

Millie was silent. Lisa looked at her in frustration then left the house, slamming the door. Millie stared out the window and began to remember a similar conversation that took place years ago.

"Where are you going?" a fourteen-year old Millie asked.

Her nineteen-year-old sister gave her hair a final pat and turned from the mirror and smiled at her little sister.

"I'm going to the club with Mack. How do I look?" Bethelee asked.

Millie shrugged. "Okay, I guess."

"You wouldn't give somebody a compliment if they paid you." Bethelee sighed. She picked up her sweater from her bed and settled it about her shoulders. "Mack said he talked the manager into letting me sing tonight. Isn't that great?" Bethelee grinned.

"Grandma won't like it," Millie said.

"She will just have to get used to it. Besides, I'm really good. Mack says that once the manager hears me, he will offer me a singing job on the spot," Bethelee said confidently.

"Grandma won't let you take it. She says it's the devil's work and she's right," Millie smirked.

"What do you know about it? Nothin'! And I don't care what Grandma thinks. If I'm offered the job, I'm taking it," Bethelee retorted.

"You'll be sorry," Mille threatened.

"I'm just sorry I'm stuck here living with the two of you," Bethelee said as she flounced out of the room.

The memory faded as Millie continued rocking. She stared out the window at the darkening sky. Millie thought how Lisa was so much like Bethelee. Only time would tell if she would have the same reckoning.

Derek is in the archive room looking at the boxes lining both sides of the row. The whole room was filled with boxes of unsolved murders. He slowly walked down the aisle as he read each box. He finally stopped and read a label more closely. It read "Patrick Chappelle – 1965 Unsolved Murder." He looked at the box beneath it which read "Richard Hendrix – 1966 Unsolved Murder." He pulled both boxes and carried them to a table. Opening the Patrick Chappelle box, he opened a file and began reading it. After a few moments, he heard footsteps and turned to see who was approaching.

"Derek!" his partner exclaimed.

"Hey, Sam!"

"I've been looking all over for you. What are you doing in here?" Sam said as he picked up one of the boxes and read the label. Derek continued reading the file he held.

"The Patrick Chappelle murder. That was some time ago," Sam asked. "Why the sudden interest?"

"It's an unsolved murder," Derek replied.

"That happened seven years ago. It's a cold case," Sam said.

"Yeah, but my sister-in-law is stirring the pot. Now Angela wants me to take a look at the file. I told her I would," Derek explained.

"She thinks you're going to find a vital clue that will solve the case?" Sam smirked.

Derek chuckled. "Something like that. How did you know?" Derek smiled.

"Lucky guess." Sam put the box down and picked up a folder. He flipped through the pages. "I'm sure the previous detectives were very thorough," Sam said. "What do you think you're going to find?" Sam asked.

"I don't know. But it doesn't hurt to poke around a little. Maybe I'll find that all important clue," Derek suggested.

"I doubt you'll find the missing link in these files. There's not much here. There doesn't seem to be much that the detectives had to work with. And if the crime scene held a piece of evidence, it's long gone by now," Sam reasoned.

Derek knew that everything Sam said was true but something just didn't sit right. He couldn't find any details in the file. Things like who was questioned? What time did the murder happen? Where were the photos of the body and description of the weapon? The information was sketchy, only saying that the weapon was probably a large kitchen knife. Nothing specific. What about the type and make of knife. Why wasn't that information in the file? Had it been lost? Was it ever here? If so, where was it now? There were too many unanswered questions that should have been addressed during the original investigation. Derek looked at Sam and knew what his reaction would be to what he was about to proposed.

"It might be a good idea to take a look at the crime scene anyway. You never know what you might find," Derek smiled wryly.

Sam was shocked.

"Are you out of your mind? It happened years ago. Whatever was there, if there was anything, is long gone. You're on a wild goose chase, my man."

"Maybe. But there are just too many holes in this investigation. I know we will find some answers if we start digging," Derek said.

"But what about the passage of time? All physical evidence will be destroyed by now," Sam said rationally.

"Maybe. But sometimes forensic evidence can survive the ravages of time. We'll never know unless we check it out," Derek said.

"We? You expect me to accompany you on your pointless venture? I think not. You're on your own with this one, my friend," Sam said firmly while folding with his arms across his chest. "I'm not getting involved. Not this time. I'm staying out of it!"

Derek looked at Sam and smiled.

"This is crazy," Sam said irritably.

Derek and Sam were in the park walking by the lake.

"Why did I let you talk me into this? Looking for old evidence that doesn't exist, in a park, of all places. I would do better by looking for the proverbial needle," Sam muttered.

Derek grinned at him. "You're helping me because you're my partner and best friend," Derek said. "And deep down, you know those detectives did a lousy job investigating this case.

"Maybe they did but this is still insane. And don't play the friendship card. I may get a new friend just to irritate you," Sam countered but somehow the threat sounded empty.

Derek just laughed. "And we have to be here because the park is where Patrick and Richard were found," Derek grinned.

"You know old Hartley and Melbourne are going to be ticked with you poking around their old case," Sam said seriously. "They're sure to think you're trying to make them look bad."

"They already look bad. If I come up with crucial evidence, they need to crawl into a hole and never come out. Look!" Derek pointed ahead of them and said. "There's the bench where Patrick was found."

"And where twenty billion people have sat since then," Sam said dryly.

"You're such a kill joy," Derek sighed. "Come on, let's take a look."

"You're lucky this bench is even still here." Sam said as he rolled his eyes.

"The city never changes anything unless it's forced to," Derek replied.

They begin examining the bench. Derek got on his knees and looked under the bench seat. Sam looked at the passing people and said. "People are looking at us like we're nuts!"

Derek continued his scrutiny. "This is Brooklyn," he responded. "People could care less about what we're doing."

Derek spotted a piece of fabric that was snagged under the seat.

"Look at this," Derek said with interest.

"What?" Sam asked.

"Get down here and I'll show you," Derek urged.

Sam kneeled beside Derek. His eyes followed Derek's pointing finger. "It looks like a piece of fabric. It appears to be pretty old and worn," Sam murmured.

Derek carefully disentangled the fabric from the underside of the bench. He stood and peered at it closely. He said, "It's still in fairly good condition. Being under the seat protected it from the elements," Derek said. "I'll take it to the lab to be examined."

He placed the fabric into a small plastic evidence bag. Sam stood up and said, "Derek, that piece of material could have been ripped off of anybody's coat. It's not likely that a piece of fabric from seven years ago would still be here. It would have disintegrated by now."

"Or it could have gotten snagged onto that protruding nail seven years ago," Derek countered. "The one thing the file did say is that the probable perpetrator was wearing a dark blue coat according to a passing jogger. And this cloth is navy blue."

"You're reaching, Derek. They are a lot of ifs in your theory. Too many for it to pan out," Sam insisted. He began pacing.

"This piece of cloth may prove to match the killer's coat," Derek said, lost in thought.

"It's a long shot, man! We don't even have a coat to compare the fabric," Sam frustration was beginning to show as he paced in front of the bench.

"True. But just hang with me on this. I've got a gut feeling that we've stumbled onto something here. Besides, we've got absolutely nothing else to go on. It's worth a try," Derek cajoled.

Sam stopped pacing and looked at Derek's earnest face. "All right. I'll trust your gut against my better judgment," Sam said resignedly.

Derek grinned. "Come on. Let's get back to the station."

Josie sat in the nursery rocker feeding the baby. She heard a door slam and heavy footsteps. She wasn't alarmed. She would know those footsteps anywhere. Rob was home.

"I'm in the nursery, Rob!" Josie called out.

He poked his head around the door. "Hey, babe!" he said cheerfully.

"I'm glad you're here. You can finish feeding little Robbie while I check on dinner," she said as she stood up with the baby.

"No can do," Robert said as he went into their bedroom. Josie followed him.

"What do you mean 'no can do'? You want to eat, don't you?" she asked as she fed little Robbie.

He went into the closest and looked through his clothes.

"It's Wednesday, my night with the guys," he said.

"Can't you skip it this week? I really need your help with the baby," she asked.

"Not tonight, baby. This is the only night I have to relax," he explained as he came out of the closest with a clean shirt and pants. He put them on the bed and began to undress for a shower.

"Like I don't need a night to chill," she snapped.

"Then take one. I'm not stopping you," he said as he pulled off his T-shirt.

"It's not that easy, Rob. I can't just up and leave without having someone to take care of the kids." she said. "I can't depend on you to be here."

"Figure it out, Josie."

"Well it would be easier if I knew I could rely on you. I don't know when you'll be here and when you won't. I can't rely on you to share the load, Rob. You may as well not be here at all for all the help I get from you!" she retorted.

He had stripped down and was wearing a towel around his waist. He looked at her hard. "We can make that happen. Just say the word!" he said harshly.

"Rob! Just stay home tonight. I need you!" she pleaded.

"And I need this night out. I've been hanging with my boys on Wednesday since the day you met me. It's what I do and I'm not about to change now," he argued.

"Things have changed, Rob. We have a newborn now. That puts a whole new spin on things. And it can't all be on me. You made this baby too. Please! Stay and help me," she pleaded.

He looked at the baby then turned away. "I'm not going to allow a baby to turn my life upside down. I'm going out," he said flatly.

"You selfish punk! When are you going to think of someone other than yourself? I would like a timeout to hang with my girls too but I can't because I have the responsibility of two children. The same responsibility that you have!" she yelled.

"Don't preach at me, Josie!" he yelled as he pointed at her. "I'm working hard for this family; trying to make things happen. I've got a plan."

"What plan? And where did you go when you were supposed to be at Mama's party? Who were you with?" Josie demanded.

The baby started to whimper. Josie put down his bottle and patted his back to quiet him.

"Take care of the baby and get off my back!" he shouted.

"Answer me," she yelled.

Rob stared at her but said nothing. As she looked at his stubborn face, the anger seeped out of her. "You knew we would have to make sacrifices when the baby arrived. And don't forget there's Kimberly. She would like to spend time with you as well," she said quietly. She couldn't believe that Rob would turn away from her and the kids. He wasn't that kind of man. He just wasn't.

He looked at Josie as she cooed at the baby. She looked tired. Downright worn out and beat. He didn't want to leave her in a lurch but he didn't want to forego his night out either. He had been looking forward to tonight all day. He'd worked really hard today and he deserved some time to just chill. He went into the bath-room and slammed the door. He would have his night and that was that. Josie would just have to get over it.

The baby started crying at the sound of the slammed door. Josie walked into the nursery and sat down in the rocker. She began rocking as she stared into space. Tears began rolling down her cheeks.

⌒

Millie sat in the parlor relaxing in an old recliner by the window. She was reading her Bible. Lisa stopped at the entrance. She sighed. She was going to the club to sing and she hoped that she and Mama wouldn't argue about it again.

"Mama, I'm gone. I have a gig tonight," Lisa announced.

Millie looked up and removed her round rimmed glasses. "All right," Millie said emotionlessly.

Lisa moved toward the front door.

"Lisa."

Lisa turned to look at her. "Yeah?" Lisa answered.

"Have you talked to Josie this week? I haven't heard from her," Millie asked.

"No. I'm going to stop by to see her tomorrow," Lisa answered.

"Hmm. It's kind of strange that she hasn't called me. We talk almost every day," Millie said apprehensively.

"She's probably been busy with the kids. Kim and Robbie are a handful," Lisa responded a little impa-tiently. She hoped her mother didn't want a long chat. She really needed to leave.

52

"Yes, they are," Millie said slowly.

"I've got to go. See you later," Lisa said in farewell.

"Goodbye," Millie responded.

Lisa hurried out of the house. She would bet her last dollar that Mama would call Josie to pry into her business. Well, it was up to Josie to keep Mama out of her personal affairs. Unfortunately, Mama could always worm stuff out of Josie. And that might be the undoing of Josie's marriage. Millie closed her Bible and picked up the telephone receiver on the table next to her. She dialed. "Hello," Josie answered in dread.

"Josie? It's Mama."

Josie had not wanted to answer the phone. She felt her mother might call. She always seemed to call at the very time when you didn't want to speak to her. Rob had left in a huff and Josie was upset about their argument. Talking to her mother was the last thing she wanted to do. Millie was very perceptive. She would sense something was off with her. She did not feel like answering twenty questions from her prying mother.

"Hi, Mama. What's up?" Josie forced normalcy into her voice.

"Are you busy? I know its suppertime. Are you and Robert eating?" Millie questioned.

"No." Josie hoped that the clipped answer would give Millie the hint that she should hang up.

"Well, I called to ask Robert if he would come over after work tomorrow. That darn pipe under the kitchen sink is leaking again. Let me talk to him for a minute. I won't keep him long," Millie said suspiciously.

So much for Millie taking the hint. Now she would have to tell her that Rob wasn't at home. But no way would she tell her where he was. That would be asking for it.

"Josie? You still here?" Millie prompted.

"Yes, I'm here but Rob isn't. He—"

Millie cut her off rudely. "Not there. Where is he? He should be home with his family. Oh! It's Wednesday night, is he out with the boys?" Millie demanded.

Josie hesitated. "He's helping a neighbor get their truck started," Josie lied. "I'll tell him about your leaking pipe when he comes home. I'm sure he will swing by there tomorrow after work." Josie hoped that would be the end of it but no such luck.

"What friend?" Millie questioned suspiciously.

"A neighbor. Nobody that you know," Josie said in exasperation.

"Oh. I see," Millie said cynically.

Josie had had enough of her mother's snooping. "Kimberly is calling me, Mama. I have to go," Josie said abruptly.

"All right. We'll talk soon," Millie answered.

Not if I can help it, Josie thought as she hung up the telephone. She did not want an interrogation by Millie any time soon. She was determined to keep her mother out of her business as much as she could. She knew she should have adopted this philosophy a lot sooner but it was never too late to start. She and Rob would work through their troubles on their own. They did not need Millie's meddling to add oil to the fire. She and Rob would be fine. It would just take a little time. Josie walked to her bedroom determined to make things right with Rob.

Robert walked out of the back door of the bar. Tonight wasn't turning out to be as much fun as he had thought. He kept thinking about Josie and the argument they'd had. He didn't like Josie being so upset with him. He had quickly realized that he had been wrong. But his stubborn pride kept him from returning home. He decided that he would call her. He turned to walk toward the phone booth a few feet away when a darkly clad figure appeared out of the blackness to stand in front of him. Robert recognized him immediately. He swallowed deeply.

"It's been a long time. Hasn't it, me lad?" the figure said affably.

"Duncan. I've been meaning to call you," Rob said with false bravado. Duncan was the last person that he wanted to speak with.

"I bet ye have. Well, I've saved ye the call. Here I am. Speak away, my friend," Duncan waved his arm in a friendly gesture.

"I wanted to talk to you about the money that I owe you. You see, I don't quite have it all. And I was hoping that you would give me more time to get it," Rob said nervously. "You know I'm good for it."

"Why, I don't know that at all, my lad. I've given you quite a bit of time already. If my associates found out I've given you a wee bit more time, well, they would all want the same kind of generosity from me. I can't afford to get that kind of reputation. It's bad for business. I'm sure you understand," Duncan said softly in his thick Scottish accent.

"Yes, I do. But I have most of it. I just need a little more time to get the rest, Lord Duncan," Rob pleaded. He hadn't forgotten to use his title, whether it was authentic or not. He knew Duncan's reputation for getting his money. He had heard the horror stories of men coming up lame and even dead. Duncan didn't play and Rob certainly didn't want to be his next victim. He had to persuade him to give him more time.

Duncan stood there attired in all black. His billowing cape was draped over a severe black suit and shining black boots. Those boots were so clean that he could see his reflection in them. He looked like a cold, menacing highwayman ready to rob unsuspecting coaches on the English roads. He was well known in certain circles for his penchant for dressing in seventeenth century garb as well as for his unorthodox banking methods. He spoke with a heavy Scottish brogue and proudly referred to himself as "Lord Duncan." No one was brave enough to address him without his title even if it was undeserved. He was very proud of his esteemed, if dubious, lineage. He expected to be treated as quality, a gentleman—as he almost always treated you. He was very courteous and graceful but he wasn't one to be crossed. It was said that his dagger had found the heart of many desperate and deceitful men. Duncan didn't care if you were an honest man that had fallen on hard times or a seasoned criminal looking to make a score. When it was time to pay up, he expected his money. And the price to pay was high if you were unable to do so. Rob wasn't sure

if Duncan's honored ancestors would approve or dis-
approve of his chosen career but he could only hope
that Duncan would remember the gentler, kinder side
of his family tree and grant him a reprieve. Rob knew
that he had taken a chance in seeking out Duncan's
charity but he had had no other choice. He had to do
something fast and Duncan's bank was the only one
that would give him a loan. His credit was far from
stellar and he had run out of options. He simply had
to pull off this venture and he needed Duncan's money
to do it. He just hoped that he would live to see the
fruits of his labor. Duncan threw his black cape over
his shoulder and put his large booted foot on a stack of
crates. Leaning on his knee, he studied Rob. He rubbed
his reddish brown beard thoughtfully, his amber eyes
never leaving Rob's face. Rob looked at the red lining
of Duncan's cape and oddly thought that his spilled
blood would match it perfectly. He shook his head. He
had to stop thinking negatively. Only positive thoughts
would sustain him now. Suddenly, Duncan stood erect
and approached him; stopping mere inches away from
his face. Rob noticed that Duncan's hand rested on the
hilt of the ancient dagger worn at his waist. Rob prayed
that he hadn't lived his last day.

CHAPTER 4

Lisa took several bows as the audience applauded enthusiastically. She grinned and waved as she noticed Angela and Derek sitting in a booth toward the back of the room. She turned to the pianist and said a few words then left the stage. The band started up a new tune as Lisa walked among the diners greeting and chatting. She finally made it to Angela and Derek's booth.

"Hi, guys," Lisa greeted them.

"Hey, girl! You sounded real good up there," Derek greeted her.

"I'm almost proud to call you sister," Angie joked.

"Ha! Ha!" Lisa responded. "What are you guys doing here? Thursday's not your usual party hard night."

Lisa laughed as she pushed Angie over in the booth to sit down. Angie playfully punched her arm.

"We don't have party hard night," Derek said.

"I know," Lisa laughed.

"Just thought we'd come out for a drink. Sandra told us your band was playing here tonight. Thought we would check out your act. You're really good, Brat," Derek complimented.

Lisa grimaced at the use of her old nickname.

"Thanks," she said with a frown.

"You know you're never going to outgrow that nickname," Angie laughed. "You got to be used to it by now. Besides, I think it's really cute."

"You would. It's not you!" Lisa said in a huff. She turned to Derek. "Since you're here, Derek, you can give me an update on what you've found out about Richard and Patrick's deaths?"

She looked at him in askance. Derek hesitated. He preferred not to talk about his investigation until he had concrete evidence. He didn't consider that piece of cloth solid proof just yet.

"Well…" Lisa prompted.

Derek saw the anticipation in Lisa's eyes. She trusted him wholeheartedly to unearth crucial evidence that would lead to the killer. He didn't want to disappoint her but he wouldn't lie to her either. She deserved the truth.

"I haven't come up with a lot yet. But I'm working on a lead. I'll see how it pans out," Derek said.

"What lead?" Lisa probed.

"Nothing that I can talk about yet. It may turn out to be a dead end. I don't want to get your hopes up and then be disappointed," Derek said seriously.

"It can't be more disappointing than hearing they closed the case without catching the killer. If you come up with anything at all, it will be more than those sorry detectives found. They were absolutely worthless!" Lisa fumed.

"Calm down, Lisa," Angie cautioned. "There's no sense in getting upset. Derek is working on it. Let's just wait and see what he finds."

"All right," she sighed. She got up and continued, "I'd better get back on stage. The band will wonder what happened to me."

"Break a leg, sweetie," Angie smiled.

Lisa gave them the peace sign and walked off. Angie turned to Derek.

"Do you really have something? Or were you just pacifying her?" Angie asked.

He reached over and caressed the back of Angie's neck.

"I have something but it's too early to say it's connected to the murders," he said. "I'm running some tests. The results should give me a clue to its validity."

"I hope it's something we can hang our hats on," Angie said.

"Or our coats," Derek said wryly.

"What?" Angie was confused.

He leaned over and kissed her neck. "Just a bad joke, baby."

Josie paced the floor of their living room. She was frantic with worry. It was three o'clock in the morning and Rob had not come home yet. Where was he? What was he doing? She kept staring at the telephone, willing it to ring. All she wanted to hear was the sound of Rob's voice giving her some crazy excuse as to why he wasn't home yet. She didn't care what had kept him out so late. She just wanted him home where he belonged. She would yell at him later for staying out so late. But for right now, she just wanted to touch him, kiss him, and know that he was safe. The doorbell rang. She practically jumped out of her skin at the sound of it. It was so late. Who could be ringing her doorbell at this hour? She was suddenly afraid. Rob had a key. He wouldn't be ringing the bell. The doorbell chimed again. She knew she must answer it but she just didn't want to. Instinctively, she knew it wasn't Rob trying to enter the house. She was even more afraid than she had been before. She didn't want to face whatever was waiting for her on the other side of that front door. The bell rang a third time. She slowly moved to the door and looked through her peephole. It was Derek and Angie. She swung open the door. The look on their faces told her all she needed to know. She collapsed to the floor.

Lisa watched the mourners from the dining room window seat. She couldn't believe it was happening again. She felt like she was having a horrible nightmare. Rob was dead. Why? How could this happened to Josie again? It wasn't fair. Lisa looked at her mother speaking to the mourners. Millie smiled. How could she smile? Her daughter had lost her husband and she was smiling. How cruel could she be? Lisa stormed off into the kitchen. Sandra and Jimmy watched the people pause and look at the enlarged photograph of Robert on the easel. Shaking their heads sadly as they gazed at Rob's image, trying to understand why he was gone.

"It's so hard to believe that he's gone, Jimmy," Sandra murmured.

Jimmy placed his arm around her shoulders. Sandra continued, "He should be here teasing Josie about overcooking the rice, not lying in a cold casket under a ton of dirt."

"I know, Sandy. I'm missing him too. He and I were like brothers," Jimmy said miserably.

"Robert was a good husband to Josie. He loved her. He may not have always known how to show it but he really loved her. What's Josie supposed to do now? How will she and the kids deal with this?" Sandra asked in concern.

"Your sister is a strong woman. She'll handle it. She did it before, and she'll do it again," Jimmy said empathetically.

Sandra pulled out of his embrace and turned to face him.

"You sound like Mama!" Sandra snapped. "Josie's not a strong woman. Not now. She's broken. Her world is shattered. She's already put one husband in the ground. Today, she had to bury a second one. How much does she have to handle, Jimmy? Why should she have to endure yet another loss? It's not fair, Jimmy. It's not fair!" Sandra outburst left her sobbing.

Jimmy pulled her into his arms to console her. He gently rubbed her back. "Life isn't fair, baby," he said sadly. "It just is. You deal with it as it comes to you. And that's what Josie will do. There will be days when she can't stop crying, days when she will shut herself off from the people who love her. She will cope with this devastation the best that she can and it will get better with time. Little by little, her days will grow lighter and the sun will shine again. Until then all we can do is be there when she needs us."

"So, life's a bitch and we're just supposed to accept it and be content?" she asked while sniffling.

He cupped her face and looked at her. "Baby, sometimes we've got no say in the BS that's thrown at us," he said softly. "We just got to suck it up and keep moving."

"This is so hard for her. I know what she's feeling. I've been where she's at. But to go through it twice? How is she going to survive the heartbreak a second time? How, Jimmy?" Sandra asked despondently.

Jimmy held her tightly as Angela approached them. "Sandra? Are you okay?" Angie asked quietly.

Jimmy removed a tissue from his jacket pocket and gave it to Sandra. She wiped her eyes. "Yes. I'm fine," Sandra said through her sniffling.

"Good," Angela said doubtfully. "The last thing Josie needs is to see you falling apart. We have to put on a brave face, even though we aren't feeling it."

"I know. You're right. I just feel so badly for her," Sandra said wretchedly.

"So do I. I'm going into the kitchen to help Lisa and Mama. Why don't you relieve Josie of having to deal with Mavis? I know Josie has heard all she can stand of her exaggerated condolences," Angie suggested.

Sandra nodded and walked over to where Josie was sitting on the couch with their neighbor.

"Do you want something to eat? There's plenty," Angie asked Jimmy.

"I'll get something in a minute. I think I'll go over and speak to Rob's brother," Jimmy replied solemnly.

"Okay," Angie said as she walked to the kitchen.

Pushing the kitchen door open, she saw Millie dishing up food to be carried to the dining room.

"Take this to the table, Lisa," Millie said. She gave Lisa a bowl of rice and beans.

Lisa took the bowl and went through the swinging door to the dining room. Angela went to the table and began slicing ham.

"I feel so bad for Josie, Mama," Angie said.

"She'll be all right. She's strong. All the Shay women are tough and resilient," Millie replied.

Angie looked at her in frustration.

"I don't know if Josie can handle this. It may be too much this time," Angie said worriedly.

Lisa entered the kitchen prepared to take more food to the dining room. She stopped to listen to what was being said.

"Josie isn't the only woman who has lost her husband," Millie said. "She'll get over it because she has no other choice. She'll move on. Just like before."

Lisa and Angie looked at their mother in shock.

"Damn! How coldhearted are you? Don't you care that Josie has lost not one but two husbands?" Lisa said disgustedly.

"Shut your mouth, girl! You're not talking to some of that trash you sing with. I'm your mama and don't you forget it!" Millie snapped.

"I don't sing with trash!" Lisa was insulted.

"Hush up!" Millie gave her a look that dared her to say another word.

Angela saw Millie's anger. Millie wasn't used to being accused of anything wrong or bad. You either agreed with her or you kept your mouth shut. Mama would not tolerate Lisa's lip and Lisa's stubbornness would not allow her to back down, even if it was for her own good. Things were getting out of hand. Angela quickly tried to make peace.

"I'm just saying—" Lisa began.

"I know what you're saying and I don't like it. And I won't have it," Millie interrupted harshly.

"Everyone is on edge. Take a breath and let's concentrate on getting through this day," Angela said reasonably.

To Angie's chagrin, Lisa plowed on to make her point. "Don't you care that Josie is hurting? She's had two husbands snatched away from her because of some crazy maniac who likes stabbing people," Lisa exclaimed. "And all you can say is that 'she'll get over it.' It's ludicrous to think that will happen so easily. It won't."

"Of course I care. Josie is my daughter and I love her. But given time she will be fine. She's strong. She's a Shay," Millie stated firmly.

"And Shay women feel pain just like everybody else. We can be fragile and delicate and experience hurt just as badly as the next woman. Being a Shay does not make us invincible to despair," Lisa retorted angrily.

Millie bristled and was about to unleash on Lisa.

"Lisa, take this ham to the table." Angie handed the platter to Lisa. "Now."

Lisa took it ungraciously. "Even Shay women have their breaking point. We ain't nobody's superwoman!" Lisa retorted.

The door swung wildly as Lisa passed through it.

"One day that girl's mouth is gonna land her in a whole heap of trouble," Millie said ominously.

Angela began making iced tea.

"Lisa's comments may not have been eloquent but I get her point," Angie said quietly.

Millie looked at Angie sharply. "You taking her side?"

"It's not about taking sides, Mama. Robert was murdered the same as Patrick. Josie is not only hurting but she feels like she's been cursed," Angie exclaimed.

"Cursed! That's ridiculous!" Millie said in shock.

"Maybe, but it doesn't stop Josie from feeling that way. After losing two husbands to a killer's knife, I understand her feelings, whether they are valid or not," Angie emphasized. She desperately hoped that her mother would understand how Josie was feeling.

"Josie will deal with it," Millie replied without emotion

Angela looked at Mille sadly and shook her head. She picked up the pitcher of iced tea and left the kitchen. Angie placed the pitcher on the table and stood there with Lisa. Sandra joined her sisters from across the room. They all noticed when Millie came out of the kitchen and moved to sit next to Josie. Millie put her arm about Josie's waist. Josie laid her head on Millie's shoulder. Millie began speaking to the mourners.

"She's an excellent actress, isn't she?" Lisa snorted.

"I don't know if it's an act, Lisa," Sandra responded.

"You didn't hear Mama in the kitchen," Lisa replied flatly.

"What was said?" Sandra wasn't sure if she really wanted to know. She knew her mother could be hard.

"She just didn't seem overly sympathetic where Josie was concerned," Angie said neutrally.

"Yeah! A far cry from what she appears to be right now. She didn't have an audience in the kitchen," Lisa said scathingly. "It was just Angie and me, so she spoke freely."

"But what did she say?" Sandra asked again.

"The age old rhetoric that Shay women are strong as an ox and that Josie would get over Rob's death and move on," Angie said tiredly.

"My God! That gets old. Doesn't she get it?" Sandra asked.

"No. That's the problem," Lisa said disdainfully.

"Looking at her now, she appears to be the epitome of the sorrowful but comforting, loving mother. You would never suspect that she is so detached from what Josie is feeling. Sometimes, I just don't get her," Angela sighed.

"You never will. Mama has her ways and we just have to accept them even if we don't understand them. She's never going to change," Sandra said sadly.

Angela nodded. She didn't know what made Millie think that she had to handle everything on her own and that she couldn't show any feelings but she knew it had a lot to do with her past. Some bad stuff happened to Millie when she was a young woman that shaped her thinking today. Her mother had had it hard but she got through it all with no support from family or friends. And her husband was a far cry from being the support, strength, and love that she needed. From what Millie let slip, it seemed he was an abuser and a drunk. No wonder she thought that Shay women didn't need a man. She only had herself to depend on and that's all she thought her daughters needed.

"Mama has a lot of mess buried deep inside of her that she will never reveal to us." Angie surmised.

"I'm not sure I want to know what she's hiding. We may be better off not knowing," Sandra grimaced.

"I do know that she loves us in her own way. And she sacrificed a lot to raise us on her own," Angela empathized.

"Yeah. Yeah. We've all heard that story a million times," Lisa said jadedly. "Daddy walked out on Mama when she was five months pregnant with me and she struggled to raise us while working as a maid in white folks' homes."

"It's true, Lisa," Angie didn't like Lisa's dismissive attitude. "And despite her faults, she did a pretty good job of bringing us up."

"Okay, I get that. But that's no excuse for having a heart that's cold as ice. It's like she doesn't care that Josie doesn't have a husband anymore. Sometimes, I think Mama wouldn't care if none of us had husbands!" Lisa exclaimed.

They all looked at each other and said in unison. "We're strong. We can do it alone. We're Shay women."

"Such is the plight of the black woman!" Sandra said.

"No, just the Shay woman!" Lisa said bitterly.

"Come on. Let's mingle before Mama sends us that 'do your duty' look," Angela said grimly.

The sisters began to speak to the guests.

Later that evening, Jimmy threw himself down on the sofa in their living room. Sandra poured two glasses of wine and crossed the room to the sofa. She handed him his glass then sat next to him.

"Thanks, baby," he said.

Sandra took a sip of the wine then laid her head against the back of the sofa.

"What an awful day." She sighed. "Can the life of a Shay woman get any worse?"

Jimmy set his glass on the table behind the sofa then pulled Sandra into his arms. She rested her head on his shoulder.

"Josie is going to see brighter days," Jimmy said softly. "It's hard to see that right now but she will. It's just going to take some time."

"Aren't you afraid? You could be next," she said solemnly.

Jimmy lifted her chin and looked into her eyes. "No, I'm not afraid. I'm not next. And neither is Derek. No one is," he said firmly.

She pulled out of his embrace and looked at him seriously.

"I think we Shay women are cursed," she said.

"That's crazy talk, Sandra. Utter nonsense," he replied.

"No, it's not. First Patrick and Richard die, now Robert. I don't think the Shay women are supposed to be happily married. We've been cursed to live our lives alone, with no husband to help us shoulder the load. We're destined to be unhappy and single," she insisted emphatically.

He grasped her shoulders. "Stop it, Sandy!" Jimmy exclaimed.

"But it's true!" she insisted. "You should be scared! I am!"

He shook her again. "It's not true! And I'm not afraid. There's nothing for me to be afraid of," Jimmy reiterated. "Nothing is going to happen to me. I'm not going to get sick! I'm not going to get shot or stabbed. I'm not going to die. Baby, you are stuck with me forever."

"Yeah! Till death do us part!"

"Sandy! Enough!" He pulled her into his embrace and leaned back against the sofa.

"You're just stressed out but that's all right. It's all right to be upset and wigged out," he said softly. "You're worried about your sister which is understandable. But don't add to your anxiety by worrying about me. I'm fine and I intend to stay that way. Stay focused, baby. Stay positive. Pray and don't let the devil in."

"You're right. I just feel so badly for Josie. I wish I could reverse what has happened. Rob would be alive and Josie would be happy," Sandra sighed.

"Well, maybe Derek will be able to bring Josie some peace by finding the killer," he said.

"I hope so."

"Did you know that Derek had reopened Patrick and Richard's case?" he asked.

"Really?"

"He's hoping to find new evidence that will solve the murders," Jimmy said.

"Is he on to something?" she asked.

"He's not saying. But Pat and Rich's murders are so similar to Rob's. I think the same guy is responsible for all three murders," Jimmy concluded.

She sat up and turned to face him.

"So if he solves Patrick and Richard's deaths then he would solve Rob's too," she said incredibly.

"It could happen, baby."

"Oh God! I hope so. I really hope so," she agreed.

"Me too, baby."

He pulled her back against his chest and gently rubbed her back.

CHAPTER 5

Josie gently closed the door to Kimberly's bedroom. It had taken quite a while to calm her down. Kim had so many questions as to why Rob had left them. How was she to answer Kim when she had the same unanswered question herself? She quietly descended the stairs and walked to the coat rack. Tossing her coat over her shoulders, she exited the house. Pulling the coat tightly around her, she moved to sit on the porch swing. She began to gently swing. She and Rob had spent many warm summer nights cuddled together on this swing. They would laugh, talk, and watch with amusement at the antics of their crazy neighbors. Sure, they were going through a rough patch at the moment, but she knew they would have worked through it. They loved each other too much not to. She just didn't understand why he had to be taken from her. He wasn't a bad person. He was hardworking and good. He was honest and fun to be with. He was good to the kids and good to her. Despite the troubles they were having, Rob was a good man. No one could tell her differently. So why did he have to die? Why was he in the wrong place at the wrong time? Why did that insane lunatic have to impale that knife through Rob's heart? What had Rob ever done to him? Nothing! Rob had done nothing to deserve his fate. Yet he was gone. Never again would she feel his touch, his kiss. Never would she listen to his breathing as he slept or hear his rapid heartbeat after making love. He was gone and she was alone... again. How she wished she could hear his voice one more time...just one more time.

"Josie!"

Josie looked around thinking she had heard her name. But the wind was blowing briskly and she realized it was just twigs and branches breaking in the wind. She pulled her coat closer about her.

"Josie!"

She stopped swinging and listened intently.

"Josie!"

It was Robert. She would know his voice anywhere, under any circumstance.

"Rob!" she said as she looked around frantically. "Rob, is that you?"

"You did me wrong. You did me real wrong. Why? Why did you do it?" Rob voice was accusatory.

Josie stood and looked toward the roof of the porch, where she thought his voice was coming from.

"What do you mean? I didn't do anything, Rob. I swear I didn't!" she replied anxiously.

"Liar!"

"No!"

"Liar! Liar!" he shouted. "I'm dead. You put me here!"

"No! No! I didn't. Why do you think I killed you? You know I didn't. You know it!" Josie pleaded her innocence.

"It was you. I loved you, Josie. Why did you do this? Why? I loved you. I loved you. Too much talk. Way too much," his voice faded.

"No! Don't go! Talk? What do you mean? Don't leave me. I didn't kill you...I didn't. Rob, come back. Please come back," she wailed.

There was silence. His voice had faded away. Josie sat down on the swing and sobbed uncontrollably. She finally stopped crying and wiped away her tears. She sat desolate and afraid. He had left her alone once again. She didn't know who to turn to. Who would believe her if she told them of tonight's occurrences? She wasn't sure if she believed them herself. Had she really spoken to Rob? And why was he accusing her of his death? He thought she was the cause of his death but she's not. Why would he think that? What had happened to him that night? She had to find out. Derek needed to track down who had killed him and why. She was not going to sit on the sidelines and wait for news. She had every intention of joining the investigation whether Derek liked it or not. She began to gently swing as she stared into the night. An owl hooted, a dog barked in the distance, the sky was darker than black ink, and Josie continued to swing.

Josie parked her white Mustang in front of the police station. She looked at the doors of the building in confusion. She'd decided last night that she wanted to be involved in Rob's investigation but now she was having second thoughts. Maybe she should just let Derek handle it. After all, he was the expert. But what if he missed something because he doesn't know Rob's tendencies or habits? It might be something small but could have a huge bearing on the case. She would never forgive herself if she allowed her cowardice to contribute to the case never being solved. With her mind made up yet again, she got out of the car and went inside the building. She approached the desk sergeant.

"I would like to see Detective Derek Adams please."

The sergeant looked at her with boredom.

"He's not here," he said dismissively.

Turning his back on her, he went to a file cabinet, pulled out a drawer, and began flicking through the files. His disinterest made Josie furious.

"Well, where is he and how long will he be gone? I need to speak to him," she demanded loudly.

The officer turned back to her. "It's not your concern where he is and I don't know how long he'll be gone," he said flatly.

"You don't know?" Josie was quickly losing her temper with this insolent officer. How he had made sergeant she would never know.

At that moment, the elevator doors opened and Derek stepped into the corridor. He overheard the exchange.

"Do your job and find out!" Josie shouted.

"Look, lady, come back at another time. He ain't here," the sergeant yelled. "You can leave a message or not. I really don't care."

His rudeness made Josie blow. "I'm not leaving a message for you to toss in the trash the minute I walk away. Make a call! Search the building. Move your sorry ass and find him!" she yelled.

Derek rushed over to the reception counter.

"Josie, I'm here," Derek said hurriedly. "I wasn't expecting you. I'm glad to see you."

Josie looked at the sergeant contemptuously.

"I thought he wasn't here," Josie said smugly. "Check your sources before giving out incorrect information."

The sergeant fumed. "Look, lady, I—"

"That will be all, sergeant," Derek interrupted him. He turned to Josie. "Let's go up to my desk where we can talk," Derek ushered Josie to the elevator. The sergeant could have happily thrown darts at her back.

Derek and Josie exited the elevator on the third floor and moved to his desk. He helped her out of her coat then seated her into his visitor's chair.

"I can guess why you're here, Josie," Derek said.

She took her coat and laid it across her lap. "I doubt that think you can," she replied.

Her answer surprised him. He sat in his chair and leaned back into it. He picked up a pencil and began to twirl it.

"What do you mean?" he asked.

"I imagined you think I'm here to plead with you to find Rob's killer. That's not exactly the reason. I want you to find Rob's killer but I want to help you do it. I intend to be closely involved in the investigation," she said confidently.

Derek stopped twirling his pencil.

"And just how involved do you mean when you say 'closely?'"

Josie took a deep breath. "Every step of the way," she said.

Derek broke his pencil in two just as Sam came to sit at his desk across from Derek's.

"Hi Josie. It's good to see you," Sam said. "I'm very sorry for your loss."

"Thank you, Sam. Maybe you can help me persuade Derek to accept my offer."

Sam raised his eyebrows but said nothing. He could tell by looking at Derek that he was not open to Josie's proposition. He sat quietly at his desk and listened to the conversation.

"It's not a good idea, Josie," Derek said kindly. "I will keep you informed, of course, but it isn't wise for you to be involved in the small day to day operations. You would only be bogged down with inconsequential things."

"It's those 'inconsequential things' that I am interested in. They could lead to a break in the case that could solve it. I can supply you with information that you would never think to ask. Information that could be relevant to the case," she insisted.

"Such as?" he responded.

"Did you know that we were in debt at the time of Rob's death? So badly in debt that we were close to losing our house?" she asked.

"No, Josie I didn't. I'm sorry," he said sympathetically.

She nodded acknowledgement of his statement. "Did you know that Rob had a plan to save us from ruin?" Josie asked.

He sat forward in his chair placing the broken pencil on the desk.

"What plan?" Derek questioned.

"I don't know. He never told me. He didn't know that I was aware of his scheme. I never told him that I knew that he had one. But its things like this that I can contribute to the case. I know bit and pieces that may lead you in the right direction. Please let me help you find the killer. I really need to do this. Please, Derek," she implored.

He looked at the tears gathering in Josie's beautiful hazel eyes. There was no way he could say no her. There was no way he could deny any of the Shay sisters. They had a way of tugging on your heartstrings to get what they wanted. And Josie was no exception. It was against his better judgment to have her so involved. It could also be dangerous, which he knew Angie would object to. But how could he say no to a woman who had lost two husbands in such a horrific way? He couldn't and he knew it. He took a deep breath.

"All right, Josie," Derek said resignedly.

She got out of her seat and bent over to hug him. "Thank you, Derek. You're the best brother-in-law a girl could have," she said enthusiastically. "You won't be sorry. I promise you won't. I've got to go but I'll be in touch soon. Call me if there are any new developments."

She kissed him on the cheek and walked to the elevator. Derek didn't miss the appreciative looks the other officers paid her. Her black mini skirt and red heels drew attention to her slim, alluring hips and sexy legs. She put her coat on as she waited for the elevator—a navy blue coat. He also noticed the torn hem. Was it just coincidence? The elevator arrived and she got on. He glanced around the office and his thoughtful expression became a warning stare of "don't even think about it" to his fellow officers. Sam grinned as he checked out Derek's scowl.

"Got your 'big brother' hat on today," he said.

"I have to. Josie doesn't realize the sensation she causes," he said grimly.

"She's totally oblivious?" Sam asked in disbelief.

"Totally."

Sam shook his head incredulously.

Derek sat back in his chair and thought about what Josie had shared. This plan that Rob had was something he could look into. As much as he hated to admit it, Josie had given him a good lead, one that he wouldn't have had without her input.

It seemed that Sam read his thoughts.

"Josie gave you an interesting lead. I think you made the right choice in bringing her on board. She can help us," Sam said thoughtfully.

"I think you're right, Sam," Derek conceded.

"She knew her husband better than anyone. Who better to ask questions of?" Sam queried.

"Who better, indeed? Let's get to work trying to unravel this plan of Rob's. Maybe it will lead us to Patrick and Richard's murderer too," Derek said as he started making notes.

Sandra and Angela met each other on the sidewalk in front of Josie's house and hugged each other.

"What are you doing here?" Angie inquired.

"Josie asked me to come over," Sandra responded.

"Same here. I wonder why?" Angela mused.

"Maybe she just wants to talk. She's been having a rough time of it," Sandra sadly said.

"Not really," Angela said.

"What do you mean?" Sandra was confused.

"It's just that the last few times I've talked to her she seemed normal. I mean downright chipper. Haven't you noticed?" Angie asked in wonder.

"Yes, but I thought she was putting up a front. Josie doesn't like breaking down in front of people," Sandra said.

"Well, we're her sisters. She knows she can show her true feelings with us. I don't think she was pretending for our sake," Angie said.

"Come on, it's starting to rain. Let's go in. We can argue the point another time," Sandra said. They ran to the porch.

Sandra pushed the doorbell. After a minute, Josie opened the door. She was pointing a large knife directly at them. Angela gasped and stepped back.

"Josie! Put that thing down!" Sandra exclaimed.

Josie looked down at her hand and grinned at them.

"I forgot I had it in my hand," Josie explained. She gestured with the knife for them to come inside. "Come on in."

"I will when you put that hatchet down. You could kill somebody," Angie cried out.

Sandra elbowed Angie to be quiet. Angie realized her faux pas.

"I'm sorry, Josie. I shouldn't have said that," Angie said miserably.

Josie was nonchalant. "Girl, please! Come on back to the kitchen," Josie said casually.

Sandra and Angie looked at each other in perplexity. Josie walked toward the kitchen. They removed their jackets and hung them on the coat rack then made their way to the kitchen. They sat at the table as Josie stood in front of the cutting board.

"I was just chopping fruit for a salad," Josie said. "I'll be finished in a minute."

"No problem," Sandra snagged a strawberry from the bowl to munch on. "You know we're always glad to come see you. What did you want to talk about?" Sandra asked curiously.

Josie continued chopping fruit. "There is something," Josie replied.

Angela and Sandra looked at each other again in bafflement. Angie gets up and goes to the refrigerator and takes out a pitcher of iced tea. Sandra moved to the cupboard and took out glasses.

"Well, are you going to tell us?" Angie said as she poured the drinks.

"I had a visit from Rob."

Josie said it like it was the most common thing to happen. Sandra and Angie were stunned. Sandra was the first to recover.

"You had what?" Sandra gasped.

"A visit from Rob," Josie repeated.

"You mean you had a dream," Angie clarified.

"No. Rob came to me," Josie explained.

"You saw him?" Sandra questioned incredibly.

Josie stopped cutting fruit and looked at them.

"No, but I heard him," Josie explained.

Sandra and Angie looked uneasy. Angie looked warily around the room.

"Are you sure you heard his voice? Maybe you imagined it," Sandra corrected her.

Josie violently stabbed the knife's tip into the cutting board. Her sisters jumped.

"I know what I heard!" Josie snapped.

Sandra eyed the knife uneasily.

"Okay! Calm down. We believe you," Sandra said hastily.

"We do?" Angie asked Sandra in disbelief.

Sandra elbowed Angie to be quiet. Josie pulled the knife out of the cutting board and stared at the blade.

"You might want to put that knife down," Sandra said quickly.

Josie looked at them indignantly. Sandra knew that Josie faulted them for not believing her. Her story was crazy but they needed to give Josie a chance to explain.

"Tell us what happened, Josie. Start from the beginning," Sandra said quietly.

Josie put the knife down and sat at the table. Angie poured her a glass of iced tea as Josie began speaking.

"One evening, about a week ago, I went onto the porch and sat on the glider. I was thinking about Rob and how much I missed him. All of a sudden, the wind became blustery and leaves were blowing all over the place. The clouds darkened and the birds began to fly away. I thought a storm was brewing. Then I heard my name. At first, I thought I had imagined it but a moment later I heard it again."

"It had to be the wind, Josie," Angie interjected.

"No. The wind was high but I know what I heard." Josie refused to be contradicted. "He said 'Josie.' He called out my name several times."

"He?" Sandra asked in foreboding. She was afraid of Josie's answer.

"Yes. Rob."

"Oh, no!" Sandra and Angie said in unison. Shock did not describe their reaction.

"Sweetie, it couldn't have been Rob. He's gone," Angie reasoned.

"It was him, I tell you. It was Rob. I called out to him and he answered," Josie said passionately. "It was him."

"Well, what did he say?" Sandra said doubtfully.

"He asked me why? Why did I do this to him? He thinks I killed him," she said pathetically.

"What? If it was him, he's nuts!" Angie exclaimed.

Sandra put her hand on Angie's arm to quiet her.

"It was him," Josie insisted. "And I told him he was wrong, that I didn't kill him. But he called me a liar."

"Oh, honey," Angie empathized.

"Why does he think I killed him? I would never hurt him. Never!" Josie choked on her tears.

Sandra got up to hug Josie as Angie grasped her hand.

"I'm sure he doesn't blame you," Sandra said softly.

"He does, Sandy!" Josie sobbed.

"Well, he's obviously confusing the issues," Angie determined. "If he thinks you had something to do with his death then we've got to figure out what he's talking about."

"Then you believe me? You trust that I really did talk to Rob?" Josie asked as she took a tissue from Sandra to dry her eyes.

Sandra and Angie looked at each other. It was really too farfetched for even an over-imaginative Josie to make up. Somehow, Rob had communicated with her and he was very angry. They had to find out why. In silent agreement, they nodded.

"We believe you, Josie. You couldn't make up something this fantastic," Sandra said.

"This is too crazy even for your fertile imagination," Angie said with a grin.

"Now we just have to get to the bottom of it. Why would Rob think you had something to do with his death? What did you do, Josie?" Sandra asked.

"Nothing!" Josie exclaimed.

"It had to be something. Why else would Rob accuse you?" Angie added.

"I don't know. But I'm telling you, I haven't done or said anything that would lead to Rob's death. He knew that I loved him too much to harm him. I still love him," Josie rationalized.

"We know you do, Josie," Angie said gently.

"Rob doesn't. He called me a liar," Josie said sadly.

"He didn't mean it. He was just mad and wanted to strike out at somebody. You were the most likely candidate," Sandra said kindly. "But he'll see reason when we find the truth. And we will find it."

"Come hell or high water," Angie smiled. "Come on. Let's look over all of Rob's papers. There's got to be a clue in them."

They all left the kitchen and went into Josie bedroom. Josie pulled out several boxes and put them on the bed. They began searching through them.

Josie paused her searching. "I asked Derek if I could help with the investigation," she said thoughtfully.

Angie looked at her and asked, "What did he say?"

"He said I could. But it probably was just lip service," Josie surmised.

"No. If he said you could help, he meant it. Maybe you'll find something in these boxes that will be useful to him." Angie said hopefully.

"Maybe. Let's keep at it," Josie said with renewed spirit.

CHAPTER 6

Millie stood at the kitchen sink washing dishes. She has always been adamant about doing them herself. She didn't trust dishwashers to do as good of a job as she could do. She looked out the window at the pouring rain and thought of another time when it was raining heavily.

A young Millie was standing in the doorway of her small house looking out at the rain. The worn wooden steps leading to the porch were soaked and sagging. Those steps wouldn't see another summer, she thought. She would have to sweet talk Leon into building some new ones. Heaven only knew if he would actually do it. If not, she would probably have to ask old Hank if he would build some new ones. Hank was getting up in age and she hated to ask him but she could depend on him—something she couldn't do with Leon. She heard a loud engine roaring above the fiercely blowing wind. She pulled her threadbare sweater more closely around her and looked down the dirt road. She saw bright headlights cutting through the gray, murky afternoon. The old truck stopped in front of the house.

Millie recognized the driver. It was Lorraine from that club in town. She leaned over and kissed Leon long and hard. The kiss finally ended and Leon got out of the car. Lorraine saw Millie and wiggled her fingers in greeting. Millie stared at her in hatred. Lorraine laughed then gunned her motor and took off. Leon ran onto the porch.

"That brazen heifer had the nerve to come to my house and kiss you right in front of me!" Millie said angrily.

"Don't you start, Millie. I ain't in no mood to hear your harpin'," he snapped.

He brushed past her and entered the house. He went into the kitchen and got a bottled beer out of the little ice box. Millie followed him to the kitchen.

"And what kind of mood do you think I'm in after seeing you with that slut?" Millie hissed. "She was kissing you like she has a right to, and you likin' every bit of it. How could you hurt me like that, Leon? How could you disrespect me that way?"

Leon sat down at the kitchen table and slouched in the chair. He took a long swallow of beer. "Shut up, Millie!" he said bitingly.

"What have I done to make you treat me like this? Why do you hate me so much?" she asked miserably.

"I don't hate you. What you got to understand is what I do outside of this here house ain't no business of yours. I takes care of you and those girls, don't I? That's all you needs to be bothered about," he said angrily.

"But—"

"Ain't no but about it! So long as I put food on the table and clothes on your boney back, you ain't got nothin' to complain about," he shouted.

Millie felt that she had put up with about as much as she could take.

"I got plenty to complain about," Millie yelled. "You don't see me goin' round with all kinds of men havin' my fun! That's cause I love you, Leon, and I wouldn't disrespect you like that."

He breaks out laughing. "Don't know any man that would want you! Look at you! Dirty dress that's seen its last day. Hair uncombed and not wearing a drop of makeup. Who you think wants to be with you?" He laughed harder.

"I been working in the yard and got pretty dirty. But I'm gonna clean up," Millie said as she ran her hand over her dress trying to smooth out the wrinkles.

"Like I said, ain't no man gonna look at you twice," Leon smirked. "Not even once."

"Not even you, Leon?"

He slammed the now empty beer bottle on the table. "Hell, no! What I want I gits from pretty women!" he yelled.

He got up from the table and went into the bedroom. Tears rolled down Millie's face as she turned to look out the window over the sink. Her hand brushed against the handle of a large knife that was on the counter. She picked up the knife and gazed at it. With knife in hand, she turned to look at the closed bedroom door.

The memory faded as Millie continued to peer out at the rain.

"Hi, Mama! I'm home!"

Lisa entered the kitchen and tossed her purse on the table. She saw her mother standing at the kitchen sink and wondered why she hadn't answered her. Lisa suspected that she was in one of her weird moods again. Millie turned toward Lisa in a daze. There's a large knife in her hand. Millie began walking toward Lisa.

"Mama! What are you doing? Stop!" Lisa backed away as she shouted.

Millie continued moving menacingly toward Lisa. Lisa panicked.

"Stop, Mama! Stop!" Lisa yelled.

Angela and Derek were in bed fast asleep. There was a loud banging on the front door. They both woke groggily. Angela then heard a familiar voice calling her name.

"Angie! Angie! Open up! Derek!"

Angela and Derek sit up in bed and look at each other in sleepy perplexity.

"Angie! Derek!"

"That's Lisa!" Angie exclaimed. Angie jumped out of bed and grabbed her robe off of the chair.

"Why the devil is she banging on our door in the middle of the night? It's after midnight," Derek said irritably.

Angela hurriedly tied her robe. "We're about to find out," she said as she ran out of the bedroom.

"Great," Derek grumbled as he reached for his robe at the foot of the bed. "Just great!"

Lisa was still pounding on the door as Angela quickly unlocked and opened it. Lisa rushed inside.

"You guys sleep like the dead," Lisa gasped. "Which is what I was about to be if I'd stayed in that house a minute longer."

"What!" Angela said totally confused.

Derek came down the stairs. "Lisa, what's got your unmentionables in a knot?" Derek asked disgruntled.

"Mama tried to kill me," Lisa accused.

"Lisa, please! You can't be serious. Mama would not kill her baby," Angie said.

"She would have had she not snapped out of whatever daze she was in. She was acting insane. I could have been dead within two blinks," Lisa insisted.

Lisa went into their living room and plopped down on the sofa. Angie sat on the sofa as well while Derek stood behind the chair adjacent to the couch.

"Lisa, that's crazy," Angie sighed. "Mama would never do such a thing. You're her favorite."

"She would and she did. Besides, Josie is her favorite," Lisa said stubbornly.

"Okay, Brat. Start at the beginning," Derek said.

Lisa told them the story of what happened when she arrived home from her gig. "I think she was having some really bad memory and mistook me for somebody else," Lisa shuddered at the thought of it.

"What did she say when she realized it was you?" Derek asked.

"Nothing," Lisa answered.

"Nothing? She had to have said something," Angie exclaimed.

"She didn't say a thing. She just put the knife down and left the kitchen. I left the house and I'm not going back," Lisa announced.

"You have to go back, Lisa," Angie said gently.

"Oh, no, I don't! Not tonight. Maybe not ever. I'm sleeping right here on this dilapidated couch!" Lisa stated. Lisa squirmed about on the sofa trying to get comfortable. "Damn! You guys need a new sofa. How do you sit on this thing?" Lisa complained.

Angie answered her dispassionately. "The same way you're going to sleep on it, if I let you."

Derek moved to the front of the chair and sat down. "I know you're scared, Brat, but I'm sure Mama wasn't going to hurt you," Derek said empathetically.

"What do you call it when somebody comes at you with a large knife? Hugs and kisses?" Lisa replied sarcastically.

"Stop, Brat. You know she would never hurt you. She's way too protective of her daughters to ever hurt any of you," Derek said softly.

"Yeah, when she's in her right mind, but she wasn't tonight. It was like she was seeing a whole different scene," Lisa said anxiously.

"A scene from her past," Angie surmised. "Probably something that happened when we lived in Mississippi. That wasn't a good time for us as a family. Mama and Daddy would have some real bad arguments when we were kids. This was before you were born, Lisa. The arguments would get so bad that I was afraid somebody would get hurt," Angie said thoughtfully.

"Has she ever talked about that time with you and your sisters?" Derek asked.

"No, but Josie, Sandy, and I remember when we saw Mama with a knife. We thought she was going to slice and dice Daddy with it. Sometimes I think she would have killed him had she not seen the three of us peeping into the kitchen from our bedroom door. She put the knife down and yelled at us to go back to bed. I can still see the hateful look on her face as she held that knife. It still makes me shiver just thinking about it," Angie shuddered at the thought. "Funny thing though, that knife she held had a funny look to it. It had kind of a hook handle. It was a strange looking kitchen knife. Not like the kitchen knives we use today." She shrugged.

"Your dad walked out on you guys, didn't he?" Derek confirmed.

Angie nodded affirmatively.

"Do you know why?" Derek questioned.

Angie shrugged.

"He was a lousy man, I guess," she answered. "I mean, what kind of man just up and leaves his wife and kids and never looks back? Apparently he only cared about himself and life was easier without his family as baggage. Anyway, one day, Mama told us that he was gone, as good as dead and he would never come back. Three months later, we moved to Brooklyn."

Angie stood up.

"Come on, Lisa. You can help me get the linen for your lumpy bed," she said.

Lisa eagerly jumped up.

"Great! I'm moving in with you, you know. I'm not going back to live with Killer Millie!" Lisa said excitedly.

"Stop it, Lisa," Angie admonished but giggled as she and Lisa left the room.

Derek was thoughtful as he returned to his bedroom. Life for Millie had been difficult. Derek was sure it had a bearing on why Millie was the way she was. Derek was getting into bed as Angela entered the room. She removed her robe and got into bed as well.

"Is Brat all tucked in?" Derek asked.

"Yes. She fell asleep immediately," Angie responded as she moved to lay her head on his shoulder. "I think feeling safe made the fears fade away."

"I'm sure it did but she knows she has to go back to the house, right?" he said.

"She knows but not tonight. Tonight she can sleep peacefully on our lumpy couch," Angie murmured. Angela promptly fell asleep. Derek remained awake, dubious thoughts swirling in his head.

Duncan sat in a dive on the outskirts of Brooklyn. It was the only bar around that served decent Scottish ale. He was sitting with his back to the wall at a small table in a dark corner. He always sat where he was able to view his entire surroundings, he wasn't one for being taken by surprise. He leaned back on the hind legs of the chair and considered his next move. Taking a swig of ale he contemplated the demise of Robert Brooks. 'Tis a shame he wasn't able to get his money out of him before his unfortunate departure. But all was not lost.

He still could recoup his funds. He simply would have to call on the grieving wife. A pleasant visit to explain his current dilemma would surely ignite her sensibilities to want to correct a wrong done to him by her deceased husband. If not, he would simply have to coerce her to see reason, by any means necessary. He smiled slowly as he raised the mug of ale to his lips. She was a choice morsel of a damsel. He fervently hoped that she would need persuasion.

Derek and Angie were in the car on their way to Josie's house. A couple of weeks had gone by since Josie had visited Derek at the station. He was extremely annoyed with the slow progress of the case. He wanted to have something positive to tell Josie when she came back but he had precious little to work with. And without a murder weapon he was left with no clues. He had not gained any ground with the information Josie had given him about Rob's plan but he was still digging. But he still had that piece of fabric he found at the park. He needed to find out what it was torn from. He had an idea but it was a long shot. If he was right, he would have created a mess he wanted no part of. Angela looked over at him from her passenger seat and smiled. He returned her smile. He knew he was a lucky man. He had a beautiful wife who would support him at every turn. But would she support him if it turned out that he was right about that piece of fabric? He would be duty bound to do his job. But would Angie understand? It could change their lives forever. Now here they were, driving to a possible suspect's house. He hated to think of Josie in those terms but did he have a choice? Angela had been adamant about coming to visit Josie. Derek hadn't wanted to but could see no way around it. Josie would want answers and he just didn't have any at the moment. And he certainly couldn't tell her about his inner thoughts.

"It will be good for Josie to have some company. She's been shut up in that house way too long. It's time for her to start mixing with people again. I'm so glad she issued the invitation," Angie said.

"Hmm," Derek muttered distractedly.

Angie looked at him and smiled. "You're completely preoccupied. What are you thinking?" she asked.

He glanced at her quickly as he drove. "Oh, nothing. Just work," Derek replied.

"Well, we're almost at Josie's place, so no more thoughts of work for a while. Okay, babe?" Angie pleaded.

He reached over and caressed her soft cheek. "I can refuse you nothing," Derek said. "All thoughts of work are on the back burner."

She kissed his palm that was cupping her cheek. "Thank you."

They arrived at Josie's home, exited the car and walked up her picturesque walkway.

"Looks like Josie's been busy gardening," Derek said.

"It's beautiful," Angie responded as she stopped to smell a late blooming rose. "The last bloom before the winter. Hmm, it smells heavenly."

They continued on and climbed the steps to the porch. Angie rang the bell. They could hear Josie inside calling upstairs for Kimberly to finish her homework. Josie was out of breath when she opened the door.

"Hi guys! Come in," Josie greeted them.

She helped Angie remove her coat as Derek divested himself of his own. Josie hung Angie's coat on the coat rack and said, "Come sit by the fire and warm up."

She hustled Angie into the living room and gestured to a comfortable wingback chair by the fire. Derek hung his coat on the rack and as he turned to enter the living room, he noticed Josie's coat hanging next to his own. He saw the torn hem and remembered having seen it when she was leaving his office. But there was another memory that was being elusive to him. Why did he feel like he had seen this coat at another time? He had a vague memory but he couldn't latch on to it. He lifted the coat hem to take a closer look. The coat was the same color blue and the material felt the same as the fabric he had found at the park. He couldn't be positive, of course. He would need to have it examined at the lab.

"Come on, honey," Angie called to him.

The sound of her voice made him drop the hem as if it were scorching hot. "Coming," he said as he cleared his throat.

He walked into the living room and stood by the fireplace. Josie sat down on the sofa and began pouring the steaming hot beverage from the lovely, antique teapot. She handed a cup to Angie.

"None for me. I think I require something of a little more substance," Derek said wryly.

Josie and Angie laughed as Derek moved to stand behind the bar across the room. He was pouring a scotch when the doorbell rang. Josie got up to answer the door. Jimmy, Sandra, and Lisa entered the house.

"Hi," Josie exclaimed. "I'm so happy you could make it."

"We wouldn't miss it," Sandra said.

There was a chorus of greetings as everyone kissed and hugged each other.

"We ran into Brat as we were walking up," Jimmy said as he hugged Lisa.

"Must you and Derek always call me Brat?" Lisa complained but there was no sting in her comment. Secretly, she rather liked the endearment.

Derek called out to Jimmy. "My man! I've got bourbon waiting for you."

Jimmy laughed and moved to the bar. He took the drink from Derek's hand. "You know me too well!" he grinned. They laughed as they drank their drinks.

"Where's Mama?" Josie asked Lisa.

"She wouldn't come," Lisa replied.

"Why not?" Josie was bewildered.

Lisa poured tea for Sandra and herself.

"You know Mama. She can be pretty antisocial when she wants to be. She just said she wasn't coming," Lisa said as she shrugged her shoulders. "It's just as well if you ask me. I can enjoy myself in peace."

"What now?" Angie groaned.

Lisa swallowed a sip of her tea. "She's complaining about my singing—again," Lisa began. "Says I'm staying out too late and hangin' with the wrong people. I keep telling her that the guys in my band are cool. They look out for me and get rid of any jerks that bother me but she doesn't believe me. She goes on and on about the club is no good for me and I'm going to get hurt."

"She's just protective," Sandra said.

"She's controlling, but not giving up my singing. She will just have to get over it," Lisa said stubbornly.

"And if she doesn't? What then?" Angie asked.

"I don't know. I can't move out. I'm not making enough money to live on my own. And I refuse to take in a roommate. Ugh!" Lisa said.

"You may not have a choice if Mama doesn't ease up. She gets determined to have her way when you try to oppose her," Josie said.

"I wonder why she is suddenly so concerned about you doing your gigs. I thought she began to support you when she saw you sing at her birthday party," Sandra said.

"Who knows? Mama may have seemed supportive at her birthday party but she's never been head over heels about Lisa singing in a band," Josie said thoughtfully. "I think it's too similar to Aunt Bethelee. Mama despised her sister's decision to sing for her living."

"Oh yeah! Her wild sister who intended to be a famous singer. I liked her the few times I saw her. Whatever happened to her?" Angie asked.

"The last time she came to see Mama, they had a terrible fight. She accused Mama of doing something that caused irreparable harm to her," Josie said.

"I remember that fight. Mama kept saying there was nothing she could do about it and she wouldn't have even if she could because her Grandma was right," Sandra said. "It had been a really bad scene. Aunt

Bethelee told Mama that she hated her and she hasn't been back since."

"I wonder what they were fighting about," Angie said thoughtfully.

"I don't know and I don't want to know," Josie quipped.

"Well, I pray that Mama doesn't see Aunt Bethelee in me. We may have a career in common but I'm my own person," Lisa sighed.

"Lisa, I know about what happened with you and Mama. I'm sorry," Sandra said. "I don't know what could have come over her."

"Whatever it was, it wasn't good. She really could have hurt Lisa," Josie said.

"I'll say," Lisa responded as she leaned forward from the sofa and pinched off of the cake that was on the coffee table. Angie slapped at her hand.

"Stop that! Cut yourself a piece," Angie admonished her.

"I would if there were a knife for me to use," Lisa retaliated.

Josie rose quickly. "I'm sorry! I forgot to bring it out. I'll get it." she said.

"Talking about your mother seems to bring on the gloom and doom. Can we discuss something else? Anything else?" Jimmy muttered.

They chuckle as Josie returned with the knife. She kneeled at the coffee table and began to slice the cake. Derek noticed the knife that she was using. It was an old knife that had a heavy, slightly hooked handle with a very large blade. He could not help but wonder about it. The police artist had drawn a picture of Rob's murder weapon. The knife that Josie was using looked very much like it. The handle shape was distinctive but many people could have the same knife; especially if it were handed down through generations. But still, it seemed prudent to look into it. The problem was getting that knife into the lab to analyze it. No way could he tell everyone that he wanted it and why. That would cause a commotion greater than he could imagine. Implications would stare Josie in the face. He could not do that without irrefutable proof. And right now his thoughts were just an unsubstantiated theory.

The doorbell rang as Josie was still cutting the cake. Josie looked in the direction of the door.

"Oh shoot!" she said.

She started to get up but Angie shooed her to stay in her place.

"I'll get it. It's probably Sam. I asked Derek to invite him," Angie said.

She gave Lisa a huge grin as she past her on her way to answer the door. Lisa decidedly ignored her.

Sam entered the living room with Angie.

"Hey, guys, it's Sam. Sam, you know everyone," Angie said enthusiastically.

Everyone said hello to him. Derek called out to him. "Hey Sam! What are you having?"

Sam moved over to the bar and greeted Derek and Jimmy. "I'll have a Screwdriver," Sam said.

"Coming up," Derek replied.

Jimmy moved over to sit next to Sandra on the sofa and began teasing Lisa. Sam watched the exchanged. Derek noticed Sam's distraction and smiled. "She a knockout, isn't she?" Derek said as he gave Sam his drink.

Sam quickly shifted his gaze back to Derek and shrugged. "She's all right," Sam said vaguely.

"All right? You haven't been able to look at anyone else since you've walked in. Admit it. You got it bad for her." Derek laughed.

"I'm not somebody she would be interested in," Sam said flatly.

"Why not?" Derek said incredulously.

"She's got big plans, big dreams. She's going to be a star. I'm just an ordinary man, an ordinary cop. She's got no time or feelings for me," Sam said dejectedly.

"You'll never know if you don't approach her. And what's wrong with being a cop? I'm one!" Derek said indignantly.

"You're different, man. You swept Angie off her feet before she knew what was happening. You guys are made for one another," Sam sighed.

"And you could be made for Lisa. You're a good man, Sam, and a damn good cop. You gotta try, man! Ask her out. She just may surprise you," Derek insisted.

Sam stared across the room at Lisa. He suddenly stood up straight and squared his shoulder. He took one step toward Lisa and Derek grabbed his arm.

"Where are you going?" Derek asked.

Sam looked at Derek like he had lost his mind.

"To talk to Lisa," Sam said in exasperation. "That is what you encouraged me to do, isn't it?"

"Yeah. Yeah. But wait a minute," Derek stalled him.

"What?" Sam asked irritably. Now that he had decided to speak with Lisa, he didn't want to waste any time.

"Take a look at that knife Josie is using," Derek directed.

Sam looked at the knife and shrugged his shoulders.

"It's a knife. So what?"

"Take a real look. Doesn't it look familiar?" Derek insisted.

Sam looked again. He slowly shook his head then stared at Derek.

"No. You're wrong. It couldn't be," Sam was incredulous.

"I hope I am but I've got to get my hands on it and have it analyzed." "And how are you going to do that?" Sam asked dubiously.

"Lisa," Derek said with a nod in her direction.

Sam was astounded.

"What!" he exclaimed. "No way."

CHAPTER 7

Derek sat at his desk studying Rob's case file. He looked at the drawing of the knife that may have slain Rob. He remembered seeing Josie use that knife so effortlessly. Did she use it to kill Rob with that same ease? He shook his head and muttered.

"I must be nuts."

"At times, I think you are," Sam joked as he sat on the corner of Derek's desk.

"I don't recall inviting you to take a seat," Derek grimaced irritably.

"You didn't but I take liberties," Sam grinned. "So, are you serious about your plan for Lisa?"

"It depends," Derek uncertainly.

"On what?" Sam asked.

"On whether I'm sure that Lisa can pull it off," Derek said grimly.

"Your idea is a long shot at best," Sam said.

Derek's phone rang. "Maybe. Maybe not," Derek said. He reached to answer his telephone. "Yeah, Adams…good. Send her up." he said into the receiver and then disconnected the call. "Lisa is on her way up.

This is an opportunity to ask her out since you chickened out last night."

"I didn't chicken out. She had to leave early for her gig. I didn't have a chance," Sam said in his defense.

"Well, now you do. Get your nerve up," Derek challenged him.

Derek then directed his gaze to the bank of elevators. Lisa exited the elevator. Sam looked down the hall and saw her approaching. He rose from his perch and swallowed his nerves, ready to make good on his course of action.

Derek stood. "Hello, Brat!" Derek greeted her.

"Hi, Derek. Will you please stop calling me that?" she frowned at him as they exchanged a hug. She looked up at Sam and saw his smile. She ducked her head shyly.

"Hello, Lisa. It's good to see you," Sam said.

"It good to see you too," she replied softly. She briefly looked into his face and was amazed at the gentleness she saw there. Sam took a seat at his desk which was directly facing Derek's. Lisa sat in the visitor's chair Derek indicated.

"I'll get right to the point, Lisa," Derek emphasized as he took his seat. "I want you to find a way to commandeer the knife Josie was using last night and bring it to me. Josie cannot know that you've taken it, of course."

Lisa's reaction was fierce. "You want me to do what?" she said loudly.

"Quiet down, Brat!" Derek cautioned her.

"You must be out of your mind. I won't do it! Why would I steal her knife? I don't need it," Lisa was incredulous.

"But I do," Derek said calmly.

"Why?" Lisa demanded.

Sam crossed his arm and smiled at Derek. This was about to get real good. His eyes told Derek as much. Derek sighed heavily. "Because I want to compare it to the sketch of the murder weapon," Derek replied.

Derek waited for Lisa's explosion. She didn't disappoint him.

"You think Josie killed Rob? You're nuts!" Lisa yelled.

"I believe you said that about yourself a little while ago," Sam muttered with a smile.

"Quiet, Sam," Derek snapped.

Lisa leaned forward in her seat and pointed an accusatory finger at Derek. "How could you think such a thing about Josie?" she shouted. "I asked you to find Patrick and Richard's killer, not pin Rob's murder on Josie."

"Lisa, please calm down. And lower your voice," Derek could see the other detectives looking curiously at him. He smiled grimly at them then said to Lisa. "Patrick and Richard's murder may be connected to Rob's. They were killed with a knife that is very similar to the one that killed Rob. I noticed that the knife Josie was using last night looked similar to the one described in Richard and Patrick's case. I want to match the impressions to the ones photographed from Rob's body. I've got to check it out. I'm not saying that Josie killed

Rob but I have to examine the knife to make sure that it's not the weapon used in any of the murders."

Lisa sat back and exhaled. She had been holding her breath unknowingly. What Derek said made logical sense but she just didn't like that the knife belonged to Josie. What if it turned out that the blasted knife was the murder weapon? What then? Would Josie be arrested because it's her knife? No way could Josie be involved in any of this. Josie couldn't kill a flea, let alone a person. No, Lisa knew she couldn't do it. She could not instigate the incarceration of her own sister. She wanted no part of it.

"No. I won't do it," Lisa said flatly.

Derek was prepared for Lisa's refusal. He knew it would take a hard sell to get Lisa to agree. He understood her resistance. The sisters were very close and they would never do anything to hurt each other. Lisa saw this task as stabbing her sister in the back, pardon the pun. He didn't think that Josie had anything to do with the murders either but he did have a theory, it was just too early to tell anyone about it. He had to change Lisa's mind. A lot was hinging on whether or not that knife was used in the murders.

"I know it's asking a lot of you," he said.

"Then don't ask," Lisa retorted. She anxiously twisted her hands in her lap.

"I have to. You're the only one who can pull this off. I'm counting on your sense of adventure and courage to help me with this case. You wanted me to reopen Pat and Richard's case, I—"

"Yes, but I didn't want you to put my sister in prison. And I will not help you do it," she said fiercely.

Derek leaned forward and grasped Lisa's hands. "I know what I'm asking is hard for you but I wouldn't ask if it weren't really important," Derek said softly. "I don't believe that Josie is involved either. She may have the murder weapon but I don't believe she used it. Sweetie, we have a chance to solve all three murders; to give closure to your sisters. I know you want that for them. I need your help, Brat. You're the only one who can do it."

Lisa pulled her right hand free of Derek's grasp and rubbed her forehead. She did want closure for her sisters. She loved them so much. But she also feared what could happen to Josie if the knife tested positive.

"Can you promise me that Josie will not become a suspect?" Lisa asked. "And what is this theory that you have?"

"Brat, I promise that Josie will be safe. I can't talk about my theory just yet. But I'm going with my gut and my gut is seldom wrong," Derek said solemnly. Derek knew that it wasn't a promise that he should make but he wanted to ease Lisa's anxiety. If that knife turned out to be the murder weapon, Josie would be the number one suspect. But he couldn't think about that right now. He had a responsibility to find the truth. And he was going to do just that. He would deal with any fallout later.

Lisa was in a quandary. She was the one who asked Derek to reopen Pat and Richard's case. She owed it to them as well as Derek to do what she could to help. But she felt sick about the prospect of placing Josie under suspicion. She hadn't missed Derek's wording when she asked about Josie not being a suspect. He answered that he would keep Josie safe. That didn't exactly answer her question. But she trusted Derek so she was going to go with her own gut.

"All right, Derek. I'll get the knife for you. But your theory, whatever it is, had better not implicate Josie."

Derek stood and pulled her out of her chair. He looked into her worried brown eyes and knew he couldn't ask her to steal from her sister. "Forget it, Brat. On second thought, I don't want you to do it. I cannot ask it of you," Derek said. "I won't put you in such a horrible position."

"Are you sure. I can do it. I may not like it but I'll do it just to prove that Josie is innocent," Lisa said.

"I'm sure, Brat," Derek said. He hugged her. She then pulled back to fastened her coat and continued, "I'd better be leaving.

I have to figure out how I'm going to get my hands on a certain knife." Lisa turned to walk to the elevator.

"I'll walk with you," Sam piped up as he grabbed his jacket from the back of his chair. "I have to go down to forensics."

Sam ushered Lisa forward as he gave Derek a quick look. Derek smiled as he watched them go down the hall. Looks like Sam had found his nerve. Now, he just had to get his hands on Josie's coat. He rubbed his chin as he thought about how he was going to do that.

Angela unlocked the front door of Millie's house. She wandered through the house.

"Mama! Are you here?" she called out.

"I'm out back," Millie responded.

Angela went out the back door to see Millie on her knees working in the flower bed. "Hi, Mama."

Millie looked up at Angela briefly then resumed digging a hole in the ground. "I know Lisa spent a couple of nights with you," Millie said. "I guess she spilled her guts about what happened a few nights ago."

Angie sighed heavily. Not even a hello from Mama. That boded ill for their for her visit.

"Well, she had to tell me why she was trying to take my door off its hinges. I've never heard such loud banging," Angie chuckled as she tried to inject a little humor into the situation but Millie was not amused.

"No reason for her to run off," Millie said defensively.

"Mama, you were stalking her with a knife. I understand why she ran," Angie reasoned.

Millie paused her planting and was silent for a few moments. Angie took a few steps closer to Millie. "Are you all right, Mama?" Angie asked gently. "Do you feel okay. We can always go see somebody."

"Like a shrink?" Millie demanded.

"No. But if you want to speak with someone, I can arrange that for you," Angie said. "Maybe you could speak with Reverend Lewis at the church. You like him."

Millie dropped some seeds into the hole she had dug. "I don't need to talk to anybody. I'm fine. Why wouldn't I be?" Millie answered sharply.

"Mama, you were brandishing a butcher knife at your pride and joy. You really scared her," Angie admonished.

Millie covered the seeds with dirt. "Nothing for her to be scared of," Millie said.

"She was scared, Mama, and from what I heard, she had good reason," Angie said softly.

"I would never hurt her. Never," Millie defended herself.

"I know, Mama, but what made you act like that?" Angie asked.

"Nothing," Millie grunted.

Typical Mama, refusing to open up the box where she had all of her feelings under lock and key. Why Angie thought that she could talk to her mother, she didn't know. Millie always closed up like a clam when she didn't want to talk about something. It would be like snatching a steak bone from a dog to get anything out of her.

"It had to be something," Angie sighed. "Did something happen to trigger a bad memory? Did Lisa say something to set you off? I know how that mouth of hers can cause a train wreck. It's me, Mama. You can talk to me."

Millie stabbed the ground with the hoe. "It was nothing, I tell you! Stop trying to make a mountain out of a pile of dirt. I didn't hurt Lisa and I never would. Leave me alone about it!" Millie was enraged. Angie took a few steps back and Millie noticed it. "What? You think I'm gonna come after you with this here hoe?" Millie snarled as she pointed the hoe toward Angie. "I might just do it if you don't stop badgering me."

"Mama, I just wanted to—"

"Don't just want to do nothing. Leave me alone. I mean it!" Millie said harshly as she slowly stood up. "If you can't find something else to talk about then leave."

Millie turned to go inside of the house.

"I just thought we could talk about this rationally," Angie said quietly.

Millie turned and threw the hoe to the ground. It landed only an inch from Angie's toes. Angie gasped and jumped back quickly. Millie stared at her with venom.

"There's your rational. Dig a hole and bury your nosey a———in it," Millie snapped.

Millie entered the house and let the screen door bang shut. Angie stared at the screen door in shock.

Duncan looked up and down the street. It was late and no one was about. He slipped behind the bushes of Josie's house, paused for one final look around then limberly hopped her front steps two at a time. At the door he slid a thin silver file from his pocket and proceeded to jimmy the lock until the bolt slid back, unlocking the door Duncan looked over his shoulder again then crept inside the house. He quietly closed the door. The house was dark and silent. He saw the stairs leading to the upper region of the house. He mounted them. One of the steps creaked as he stepped on it. He stopped to see if the sound aroused anyone. It had not. He softly ascended the rest of the stairs without making any more sounds. He turned to look down the hall and saw a soft yellow light coming from a doorway down the corridor. He needed to know who was in that lighted room. He began walking softly down the hall. He quietly opened the first door he came to. The soft muted blue night light made it easy for him to see the young daughter sleeping soundly. He closed the door softly. He could see another dim light shining from a room. This most certainly was the infant's room. That meant that the light coming from the well-lit room must be Josie's bedroom. He grinned as he thought about the surprise his visit would be. She would be shocked to death. Well, hopefully not literally to death. He would never get his money should that occur. He silently approached her room, peeked inside then dashed to her bed and covered her mouth before she could scream. Well done, he thought as he looked down into her frightened eyes. She had such beautiful hazel eyes. A man could get lost in those glimmering orbs. He had landed atop of her. His massive body covered every inch of her. He rather enjoyed the sensation that ignited his body but this was not the time to investigate his reaction to her. He put his forefinger to his mouth to indicate that she should remain quiet. He slowly drew his hand away from her mouth. She promptly opened it to scream. He immediately covered it again.

"Really, Mrs. Brooks? I would much rather converse pleasantly with you instead of covering your mouth in such a threatening manner. If you would kindly promise me that you will not scream the house down, I will gladly remove my hand from your lovely mouth. Have I your promise?" he asked nicely.

She nodded her head affirmatively. He slowly removed his hand from her mouth.

"Quiet now," he cautioned. He reluctantly retreated to sit on the side of her bed. He noticed that she had been reading a book and he cavalierly picked it up to peruse the cover. He smiled knowingly. "Nothing like a sensual romance to send one into the snug arms of slumber," he murmured. "It will certainly ignite pleasant dreams. Well, I will try not to keep you from your book for too long."

He tossed the book aside. He looked back at the door and walked over to close it. He then returned to sit comfortably on the bed.

"Now, we can chat without waking the children, yes?" he asked with a grin.

Josie thought she had fallen asleep and was having a nightmare. This crazed man out of the eighteenth century, from the look of his clothing, was sitting on her bed and expecting to have an amiable conversation with her. He must be mad! Oh Lord! Save me!

"There's no need to be afraid, Josie. I can call you Josie, yes? You see, I hope that we can be friends. And friends do not stand on ceremony. It's so less formal and stuffy that way. Don't you agree?" he said affably. He really did want to put her at ease. Their continued association would be much more agreeable if they could be pleasant with each other.

"What do you want? I have nothing of value here. Please, just leave and I won't call the police," she begged.

He chuckled. "You will not call the police, anyway. And you most definitely have something of value," he mocked.

"Who are you?" Josie could barely breathe the question. Her voice seemed to be caught in her throat.

He crossed one muscular leg over the other, boy style. "You can call me Duncan," he introduced himself. "Your late husband and I were business associates. Unfortunately, he died before we could complete our transaction; which brings me to you."

"Me?" Josie squeaked as she sat back farther against the pillows.

"Yes. You," he smiled.

His Scottish accent was very pronounced and at any other time Josie would have been drawn to it. But the only thing she could think of at the moment was how she could save her neck, for surely he intended to break it.

Duncan rested one arm across his stomach while he braced the other elbow atop it and rubbed his chin. He stared into space for a moment as if in deep thought. Then he looked at her keenly. "You see, your husband owed me money, a rather large sum of money. But he dinna pay me back," he said slowly. "That disappoints me greatly. But I figure there is still a chance for me to salvage our agreement despite his sudden demise. This is where you can rectify your husband's oversight."

Josie pushed against the headboard as much as she could. There was nowhere she could go to escape this nightmare. She looked at Duncan in total fright and despair. She had no idea of what he was talking about. Rob had not mentioned so much as an inkling of this business deal he had with Duncan. Obviously, he died before he could pay him back and now Duncan expected her to settle Rob's debt. He probably killed Rob for lack of payment and if she couldn't give him the money, he would most likely kill her too. My God, she was as good as dead! He looked at her expecting an answer. If only she had one. But she had to say something, anything, to placate him and get him to leave her house.

"I...I...will have to get back with you," she stammered hesitantly. She could have kicked herself. As if he would accept that answer and walk away. From the look on his face, he was ready to strangle her. Duncan's look of fury was evident in his fiery, crimson-gold eyes. Josie could see the golden specks shimmering in his angry red gaze. His eyes were beautiful. Too bad they were set to murder her!

"Mayhap I wasn't clear enough," he said. His intent gaze never left her face. "See you, I want my money and you, being Robert's surviving wife, are going to repay me. Capisce?"

He had bent toward her, placing both arms on either side of her, effectively imprisoning her. His nose was barely two inches from hers. His minted breath scorched her face as his hot eyes bored into her own. There was no brooking his intention if she didn't agree with him. She quickly nodded her head affirmatively. He pulled back and casually leaned across her bed with his forearm and hand supporting his head.

"Good," he said conversationally. "Now one hundred thousand dollars is a lot of money, I know. So—"

"A hundred thousand!" Josie exclaimed.

"Yes. Your Robert had big plans. 'Tis such a shame about his death, I believe he was on to something. Anyway, I will allow you three weeks to secure the funds and then…I'll be back," he concluded.

"But…"

"No buts. I expect to receive my money when I return, and you will not disappoint me. I will even forgive the interest to make things easier for you. I know this is a difficult time for you. Your loss must weigh heavily on your pretty shoulders. I am not a hard man. I understand your plight and have empathy for you. But I am a businessman and as such certain transactions must be settled…one way or another." He smiled as he stood up and adjusted his cape.

Josie was stunned. "How do I contact you?" she asked in despair.

"You don't. But never fear. I will be in touch. Oh, one more thing. Do not go to the police. That would necessitate things getting a bit nasty…and we wouldn't want that," he said as he bent to raise her hand to his mouth. His kiss seared the back of her hand.

"Sleep well, my beauty," he murmured.

Then he was gone.

Josie sat there unable to move. Had she dreamt what had just happened? No. She still felt the lingering heat from his sensual caress. She covered her hand with the other, unwittingly trying to retain the lasting effects of his kiss. He had been there all right. His formidable presence could not be ignored or forgotten. One minute he was lethal and cunning, the next he was charming and sexy. She reluctantly admitted that she was drawn to him despite her fear of him. There was an element about him that made her want to delve deep within him to discover what was beneath the emotional layers he secreted from others. His uncommonly colored eyes drew you into his soul, although she wasn't sure he really had one. His eyes were magnetic, pulling her in, swallowing her whole. However, common sense told her that she was in a terrible situation and she couldn't even go to the police. He would surely kill her if she did. Dear Lord! How was she going to raise one hundred thousand dollars? And what had Rob been involved in that he needed that kind of money?

"Oh Rob! What have you done?" she wailed aloud.

She didn't know what she was going to do but she had to come up with something or she would be just as dead as Rob.

CHAPTER 8

Duncan sauntered down the darkened street. Everyone was abed, probably snoring in their deep sleep. He looked at the tall buildings, bright and shiny in the day, dark and somber at night. Deals were made in these buildings, deals that made some people rich and left others searching for a way to survive. He looked at their silhouette eerily fingering the smoky, heavy clouds in the sky. It would soon rain and rain hard, pounding the earth like a drummer relentlessly beating his instrument. He increased his pace not wanting to be caught in the downpour. He smiled mirthlessly as he inhaled a drag from his cheroot and thought about his previous encounter. It had been a delightful meeting. The widow Brooks was a delectable piece of baggage. Even as fear racked her body, she had still been aroused by him. He had felt it when he was laying the full length of her. It wasn't only fright that held her immobile, it was desire too. Maybe she hadn't recognized it because she was so frightened but he had, for he felt the same craving for her. He could have easily kissed her long and hard and she would have soon returned his caress just as eagerly.

The insatiable longing was there, tangible and insistent. It was summoning them to answer the desirous call. It may be insane to be craving the woman you may have to kill but he did want her; and he just may have to satisfy the yearning.

Lisa parked in front of Josie's house. She leaned her forehead on the steering wheel and sighed. Thank God Derek had released her from her promise to steal Josie's knife. She must have been insane to agree to such an act. Josie was her sister whom she loved beyond measure. And she knew in her heart that Josie was innocent. She leaned back against the car seat and looked through the rain-soaked passenger's window at Josie's house. It was just an ordinary house with an ordinary woman living inside of it. No way could Josie have killed her husband. It was ludicrous. Josie wouldn't harm a flea. Derek was reaching for straws but she wasn't going to help him nail her sister to the wall. She sighed as she got out of the car and opened her umbrella. She ran to the porch and rested her opened umbrella near the door. She rang the doorbell.

Josie heard the doorbell and thought whoever it was had horrendously bad timing. She had awakened rattled and irritable. Her mood was as dark and gloomy as the rainy day. She could not stop thinking about last night and how her life had turned upside down. Lord! What had she done to live this horrific dream? Kimberly had been in a bad mood too. She was uncooperative in getting dressed and refused to eat her breakfast. You would think she would have been excited for her visit with her friend, Jasmine. It had taken over two hours to get her dressed, fed, and waiting at the door for her friend's arrival. Jasmine and her mother Hannah had finally arrived and they were off to the aquarium. Maybe seeing all of the sea life would put Kimberly in a better mood. Unfortunately, there wasn't much that could improve her temperament. Josie shut the door after the last goodbye and dragged herself to the kitchen for a cup of coffee. She had to focus on her problem and figure out what to do. She poured the coffee then slumped in the kitchen chair. Lost in thought, she absently spooned so much sugar into the cup that she couldn't drink it. She pushed it aside and closed her eyes. Where was she going to get one hundred thousand dollars from? The only money she had was Rob's insurance policy. She had used some of the money to pay off nagging debts. She loathed using the remaining money for she was saving it for Kimberly's college fund. If she used it, how would she ever replace it? Besides, it wasn't enough to cover Rob's debt anyway. Did Duncan not understand that she shouldn't be responsible for her husband's actions? Until last night, she hadn't even known about this very unconventional deal, though she had the feeling that Duncan could care less about ethics. He just wanted his money and would use any means available to him to get it. She was a means to an end. She could always tell him she just couldn't get the money. What could he do? He couldn't get blood out of a turnip...but he could snatch her out of existence. He could make her disappear and no one would know what had happened to her. She shivered. Would he really do that to her? Would he kill her without a second thought? It wasn't a risk she was willing to take. She would just have to use the insurance money. She had put it aside for Kimberly's college education but she would figure something else out for her. She had time. Kim was only nine but it galled her to have to use it this way. It wasn't enough to cover the debt but perhaps it would buy her some more time. The doorbell rang again, jarring Josie back into reality. She hurried to the front door and opened it, half expecting Duncan to be standing there. Her face dropped when she saw it was Lisa.

"Oh, it's you." Josie stepped aside allowing Lisa to enter.

"Gee! I'm glad to see you too," Lisa said in a huff.

"I'm just preoccupied," Josie said as she closed the door. "What brings you here on such an awful day? Come on back to the kitchen. I'm having some coffee. Do you want some?"

"Hot chocolate," Lisa said.

They entered the kitchen and Lisa took a seat at the table. Josie retrieved a mug from the cupboard and set about making the hot chocolate. She forced a little gaiety into her voice.

"So, what brings you by?" Josie asked.

Lisa knew that this question was coming and she decided to tell Josie what was on her mind. "I'm thinking about moving out," she explained. Lisa realized moving into her own place was her only option; but she hadn't figured a way to afford it on her own. But Josie was intrigued as she knew she would be.

Josie leaned forward, her face alight with excitement. "Details. What brought this about?" Josie asked.

"I need my privacy. I'm twenty years old," Lisa said.

"Oh really? What's his name?" Josie grinned.

"It's not like that. There isn't a man involved," Lisa grumbled.

Josie's face dropped. "Oh. Well, what then?"

"It's just that Mama's been acting so weird and I'm really beginning to feel uncomfortable there. That butcher knife episode really freaked me out," Lisa complained.

"I'm sorry, Lisa. Have you talked to Mama about it?" Josie asked.

"Oh no! Angie tried that and got a garden hoe thrown at her," Lisa exclaimed.

"What!"

"You hadn't heard?"

Josie shook her head negatively.

"Angie went over to Mama's and asked her about the 'butcher knife' incident and she acted like nothing strange had happened," Lisa explained. "When Angie persisted, Mama got mad and threw the garden hoe at her; telling Angie to leave her alone," Lisa concluded.

Josie was in shock. "She actually threw the hoe at Angie?"

"She did." Lisa nodded. "And was not the least bit remorseful," Lisa said disgustedly.

"Angie must have been frightened," Josie said empathetically.

"Frightened isn't the word. She ran out of there like a bat out of hell," Lisa sat back with her arms crossed.

"I have to call Angie to see how she is," said Josie.

"Now you see why I want to move. Mama isn't herself and she won't say what's going on with her. I'm walking around on eggshells in that house. I don't know what will set her off."

"Well, moving out will certainly set her off," Josie reasoned.

"Probably so, but I'll feel a whole lot safer. I just hate to leave Mama if something is really bothering her. I'm not trying to abandon her. I'm just a little afraid of her right now," Lisa said miserably.

Josie reached across the table to touch Lisa's arm. "I know you wouldn't abandon Mama," Josie said softly. "You're in a difficult position but you have to think about your own welfare. I don't want you hurt, Brat."

She used Lisa's nickname affectionately. She loved her little sister immensely and would do anything she asked of her. She did not want anything bad to happen to Lisa.

"But this idea of my moving is probably a moot point because I don't make enough money to live on my own," Lisa said sadly.

"What about getting a roommate to share the expenses?" Josie asked.

Lisa shook her head emphatically. "I tried that when I was in college for a year. I came close to strangling the girl. I just need my own space," Lisa said sighed.

"I have an idea. What if you came to live with me? You could pay a couple of the utility bills, which would really help and I would have somebody over the age of nine to talk to," Josie suggested.

"Are you sure? I know you've wanted your privacy since Rob passed," Lisa questioned.

"I would welcome the company, Lisa. I'm just rambling around in this big house all alone, except for the kids. You would really be doing me a favor," Josie insisted. She had another reason for wanting Lisa to move in but she wouldn't tell her about it. Since Duncan had showed up, she didn't want to be in the house by herself. Maybe Lisa's presence would keep him at bay.

"Are you serious?" Lisa asked in excitement.

"Yes," Josie grinned. She would enjoy having Lisa here.

"Oh my God! Yes! Yes! Yes! I would love to move in!" Lisa jumped out of her chair and wrapped her arms around Josie's neck. "Thank you, Josie! Thank you so much."

"You're welcome, Brat," Josie said with a grin. She disentangled her neck from Lisa's tight bear hug. "And Mama won't be bent out of shape if you're moving in to be with me. I am the grieving widow, you know."

"Oh, it's perfect! Absolutely perfect!" Lisa was euphoric.

Little Robbie began to cry.

"I think someone is awake," Josie said. "He's probably wet and hungry. I'll change him then bring him down. You can feed him."

"I would love it," Lisa grinned.

"Be right back," Josie replied as she left the kitchen.

Lisa sat there grinning as she thought about her upcoming move. She looked out the window and saw out of her peripheral vision the knife block. She was glad that Derek had changed his mind about having her swipe the knife. Josie had generously opened her home to her. No way could she do something that might implicate her in Rob's murder. Derek would have to find another way. He's a cop. He would think of something. She sat back and daydreamed about her new living digs. She would go home and tell her mother about her move this evening. She hoped Mama would take the news well. She didn't want to have to dodge any flying objects to get out of the house. Mama knew that sooner or later she would be moving out. It's just sooner rather than later. She would be okay. After all, she would be helping her grieving sister, so Mama couldn't complain about that. Lisa sighed contentedly. Everything was working out perfectly. Life really could be good.

Millie sat in her favorite recliner in the living room as she roped yarn into a ball. She leaned her head against the chair back and closed her eyes. She didn't need to see what she was doing. She had been wrapping yarn since she was four years old. Her grandmother had taught her to knit early on in life and she's been knitting ever since. It was peaceful and soothing. She would always turn to knitting to ease her mind. She remembered the day she had confronted Leon down at the club. She had been knitting some gloves for the girls. He came out of the bedroom with his coat on. It was obvious he was on his way out—again.

"Where are you going, Leon?" she asked tentatively.

"Out," he said shortly.

"Out where?" she pursued.

"If you must know, I'm goin' down to the club; like you didn't know," he sneered.

"Stay here with me and the children. We could all have dinner together," she suggested.

"Why would I want to do that? I's seen enough of those young'uns for one day. I needs to go have me some fun," he said harshly.

He headed for the door. She hastily put her knitting aside and stood up.

"I'm gonna feed the children and put them to bed," she said hurriedly. "I thought you and me could spend the evening together."

She smoothed the wrinkles from her dress and nervously clasped her hands before her. He looked at her from her head to her feet. He then laughed. He slapped his knee in uproarious hilarity. She smiled hesitantly; not knowing what was so funny but she wanted to please him so she went along. He finally composed himself.

"You think I want to stay here with the likes of you? Naw, sugar," he sneered. "I'm gonna go where I can enjoy the pleasures of a real woman—a fine woman."

He started laughing again as he opened the door and walked out of it. She heard the old truck start up and rumble down the road. She slumped back into the chair in despair. How could he speak to her like that? He treated her like she was garbage, dirt under his feet. What had she done to deserve that kind of treatment? She was good to him. She cooked for him. She cleaned for him. She took care of him when he was sick. She looked after his children. She gave herself to him whenever he took a notion. Why did he treat her like she was nothing? He treated her like an old hag who kept his house, instead of a cherished wife whom he loved. She sat there for a while with eyes closed. Suddenly, her eyes popped open. She made a decision. She got up and went to the girl's bedroom. Looking inside, she saw Josie sitting by the window reading a book. Josie looked up from her book when she saw her.

"Josephine, watch your sisters for a while. I have to go out," Millie said.

"Where are you going, Mama?" Josie said.

"I'm going into town but I won't be long," Millie replied.

"I heard Daddy talking to you. Is he going with you?" the child asked.

"No. He went out," Millie said shortly. She wasn't going to try to answer the questions in Josie's eyes. "Now watch your sisters. I'll be back quick."

She left the bedroom and walked down the short hallway to grab her coat off the hook by the front door. She put it on and left the house. Millie walked briskly down the road. Determination was written all over her face. Soon Millie was standing in front of a crowded club. There was loud music and laughter coming from inside. She entered the club and stood for a moment for her eyes to adjust to the dark, smoky lighting. She weaved her way through the laughing, kissing men and women. A laughing man grabbed her waist and spun her around.

"Let's dance," he said drunkenly.

She pushed him away and shoved her way through the throng of humanity. She stopped when she saw Leon. He was sitting at the bar with a woman on his lap. She was busy kissing his neck as he drank from a tall glass. He swallowed then slammed down his glass.

"Ahh! Belle baby! You's good at pleasin a man!" he whispered in her ear. He groaned as he caressed her back. He then turned her head and covered her open mouth with his own. He then slid his hand down her stomach and under her skirt. She moaned in pleasure as she widened her thighs.

Millie had imagined what Leon was doing when he came down to the joint but seeing it with her own eyes was more than she could take. She was blinded by anger as she leapt at the woman, pulling her off of his lap and onto the floor. Belle screamed. Leon watched what was happening in shock. He looked at Millie.

"What the hell are you doing here?" he yelled.

"What the hell are you doing whoring around with that bitch?" Millie yelled back. She was breathing hard. Anger and misery consumed her.

People had seen and heard the commotion. They were watching with obvious interest and amusement.

"I'm where I want to be, doing what I want to do," he shouted at her.

Belle was sprawled on the floor. Leon stood up and bent down to help her up. She put her arm around his shoulders and stared smugly at Millie.

"You should be at home with your children and me, your wife," Millie put emphasis on her words for his benefit as well as that tramp hanging on his shoulder.

"You're married to that old hag?" Belle asked as if she didn't know. "No wonder you're here with me.... every night."

Millie raised her hand to slap her but Leon caught her wrist in midair and squeezed it hard.

"You're hurting me," Millie screamed in pain.

"Good," the woman smirked.

"Hush, baby," Leon cautioned Belle. "Go home, Millie. You don't hardly belong here."

He dropped her wrist.

"Neither do you. Come home with me, Leon. Please," she pleaded.

He looked at Millie for a few moments. Belle saw his hesitancy. She lifted her mouth to his neck and kissed him.

"Get away from him!" Millie screamed at her.

"Leave her alone, Millie," Leon demanded.

Belle just smiled arrogantly at her. Millie looked at Leon and begged.

"Please, Leon. The children need you. I need you. Come home with me."

"No," he said with finality. "I'm already at home."

He encircled Belle's waist and turned his back on Millie. As they walked away, Belle looked over her shoulder and smiled slyly at Millie. Tears finally rolled down Millie's face as she turned and left the club.

The memory faded as Millie wiped her wet eyes. She continued to wrap the yarn. Lisa came down the stairs with two suitcases. She set them on the floor and turned to face Millie. Millie looked at her dispassionately.

"You're all packed," Millie stated. It really wasn't a question.

It had been several days since Lisa had announced to Mille that she would be moving in with Josie. The big reveal had not gone well at all. Millie had insisted that Josie was doing well and there was no need for Lisa to move there. Lisa had held her ground, even getting Josie to speak to Millie. It had all been to no avail. There was no changing Millie's mind. So, the move had turned into a hostile affair.

"Almost. A few things wouldn't fit into my suitcase. I'll come get them later," Lisa said quietly, hoping the tone of her voice would keep Millie calm. She looked at Millie in concern and asked. "Are you going to be all right? I know this is sudden and all," Lisa asked.

"I'll be fine. You're not the first person to walk out on me," Millie stated.

Lisa sighed. That was a dig, a reference that Daddy had walked out on her and Lisa was doing the same thing. She was beginning to think that Daddy had a side. There were always two sides to every story. Mama had depicted Daddy as an abusive, overbearing, cheating man. But had she pushed him into another woman's arms? She had accepted Millie's description of past events at face value. But now she wondered if her mother had driven her daddy away. The same way she was driving Lisa away. It was worth considerable thought. Lisa refrained from making a comment. Instead, she picked up her suitcases and headed to the door.

"You're just going to walk out that door and forget everything I've done for you," Millie challenged her angrily. "Is that how you show your appreciation? I raised your sorry butt all by myself. I fed you! I put clothes on your back. I struggled to keep you in private school. And this is how you repay me? You're just going to leave and let the door slam behind you?"

Lisa turned to face her. She had been hearing Millie's lamentations from the day she had told her she was moving. Lisa had explained why she leaving, without actually telling her the primary reason. But that wasn't good enough for Mama because Mama was selfish. She didn't care about Josie and what she was going through. She was only thinking about herself and her unreasonable need to control everything and everybody. Too bad about Josie losing a husband—she was strong, she would get over it. Mama's needs were more important. She wanted to keep Lisa under her thumb and rule her life. Yeah! Daddy had a side.

"You know why I'm moving in with Josie. Why can't you understand that? Josie needs me and I want to be there for her," Lisa replied as calmly as she could. Controlling her temper was becoming a challenge for her.

"You can be there for her without moving in with her!" Millie's voice was growing louder and louder. "You can comfort Josie without living with her."

"I want to be there," Lisa restrained her voice.

"Why?" Millie snapped.

"Mama, we've already been over this. You know the reason." Lisa didn't understand why Millie refused to accept a perfectly sound explanation as to why she was moving.

"What I know is that you want to get the hell away from me, don't you? You don't want to live with me anymore. Think I'm going to hurt you or something. That's your real reason!" Millie yelled.

Lisa's patience snapped. "You're right, Mama! I don't want to be here! I don't trust you anymore," Lisa bit out. "You're acting strangely and doing dangerous things. We asked you what was wrong and you denied there's a problem. Yet you go around pointing butcher knives and pitching garden hoes at people. I can't stick around to be your next victim. I'm getting the hell out of here!"

Millie rose up out of her chair. She took several steps toward Lisa.

"Don't you talk to me like that! Don't you treat me mean! I won't put up with you treating me mean!" Millie said menacingly.

Lisa moved backward in fear. At that moment, Josie was on the porch. She heard some of the conversation and frantically searched her purse for the house key. She knew things had gotten out of hand. Finally, she found it and hurriedly entered the house.

"What's going on?" Josie asked anxiously.

There was only silence from Lisa and Millie.

"Mama? Lisa? I heard you arguing. Why were you fighting?" Josie insisted.

Millie looked at Lisa hard. Lisa could have sworn there was smoke coming from her ears. Millie was so angry it was palpitating in the air.

"Mama doesn't think I should leave. But I'm going anyway," Lisa said stubbornly. She hurried out of the still opened door.

"Mama, I really do need Lisa with me right now. I need her help with the kids and I need her company. It gets real lonely in that house now that Rob is gone," Josie said softly.

Millie just looked at Josie in anger then walked out of the room and up the stairs. She stopped midway up the flight.

"Close the door on your way out," Millie said without turning to look at them.

Josie sadly watched her mother ascend the stairs. Millie was a hard, cold, oftentimes unreasonable woman. It was her way or her punishment. There would be major fallout behind this incident. Mama thought that she had been wronged. There was no way she would accept it laying down. Revenge was on its way. Heaven help her and Lisa.

CHAPTER 9

Derek entered his house in a foul mood. Nothing had gone right today. He flung his jacket onto the chair and crossed to the bar. He poured a straight up scotch and downed it in one swallow. He was pouring himself another when Angela entered from the kitchen. She went to him and kissed him on the cheek.

"Hey, baby! I'm glad you're home."

He only grunted and swallowed another swig of his drink. She looked at him in alarm.

"What's wrong? This is so uncharacteristic of you. What happened?" she asked.

He walked over to the lumpy sofa and slouched on it. He took another swallow of his drink. Angie was very concerned. She sat next to him and rubbed his arm.

"Come on, babe," she said softly. "Tell me what's wrong. It's obvious something is bothering you. Tell me."

He leaned forward to put his drink on the cocktail table in front of them. Resting his elbows on his knees, he held his head with both hands.

"Everything is wrong. I promised Lisa that I would solve Patrick and Richard's murders but I've come up with nothing. It's been a month and I'm no closer to solving the case than I was when she asked me to look into it," he said in frustration.

"Oh, honey, you're being too hard on yourself. It's going to take time to find what the other detectives missed," she laid her head on his shoulder. "The missing link was hidden, never to be found. It's going to be difficult to unearth but you will. Just give it more time."

"I don't want to disappoint Lisa. She thinks I'm some kind of superhero that goes around righting all the wrongs in the world. I guess I don't want her opinion of me to change," he admitted shamefully. "I must have the biggest ego in the world."

Angie positioned her chin to rest on his shoulder. She chuckled. "Well, it is a bit overinflated," she teased.

He sighed and leaned against the back of the sofa. He covered his eyes with his forearm.

"Baby, you have some clues. You just have to piece them together," Angie continued.

"I have a piece of old cloth that could have come from anyone's coat. Not a whole lot to rest a case on," he muttered. "I've decided against asking Lisa to get Josie's knife, which means I'll have to subpoena it. I didn't want to go that route. It will only upset Josie and the knife may not even be a match," he was excessively exasperated.

Angie sat in thought for a moment. She had a sudden thought and dawning crossed her features. "Didn't you tell me that you needed to test Josie's coat to see if the fabric was a match?" she asked.

He removed his arm and looked at her with suspicion.

"Yes, but I told you that in confidence, Angie."

"I know. And I haven't repeated it. But you need to match the knife and Josie's coat, right?"

"Yeah," he replied warily.

"I'll do it. I'll get you the knife and Josie's coat," she said with confidence.

He sat up straight and faced her.

"Oh, no, you won't," he said adamantly.

"Why not?" she asked.

"I won't hear of it," he said flatly.

"Why not?" she repeated.

"For the same reason that I decided not to use Lisa. You are Josie's sister and I don't want you involved," Derek retorted.

"But I'm offering, Derek. I can get you the knife and the coat," she said. "Are you hesitating because you don't think that I can do it? Am I not as clever and daring as Lisa?"

"It's not that simple. Lisa is…um…Lisa is…"

"What? More valiant than I am. More adventurous? Courageous? Bold? What?" Angie was getting miffed.

Derek knew he'd better say something to pacify her.

"I just don't…" he realized that he couldn't think of an explanation that would not offend her. He did feel that Lisa was a little more adventuresome and risk-taking than Angela. He had thought that Lisa was better suited to handle the task. But he didn't want to tell Angie that. As he looked at Angela's mutinous face, he realized that he was being unfair. He knew that Angie could do it every bit as well as Lisa, he just had not wanted to put Angie in the line of fire if Josie caught her. That may have been unfair to Lisa but she would have been able to handle the situation if she were caught. Looking at Angie, he knew that she would be able to manage any misfires just as well. He had under estimated her.

"I love you, babe but no. Leave the detective work to me. I'll find a way to get what I need," Derek said softly.

"But I want to help you," Angie begged.

Derek grasped her wrists and held them in his lap. "You help me everyday by just being my wife," Derek smiled gently. "That's all I need from you. I can take care of the rest."

"It doesn't seem like enough this time," she said sadly.

He slid his arms around her waist, pulling her close to him.

"It's more than enough. Have I told you lately that I love you?"

She grinned. "I don't believe you've said it today," she said with thoughtful pretense.

"Well, I do love you; more than I'll ever be able to say," he murmured as his mouth drew closer to hers.

"I love you too, Derek."

He covered her lips in a kiss that lasted late into the night.

Josie sat on the bed in the guest room and folded the T-shirts that Lisa were pulling out of her suitcase.

"Did it ever occur to you that you wouldn't have wrinkles in your clothes if you folded them instead of tossing them all which ways into your suitcase?" Josie questioned with a smile.

Lisa turned from the opened dresser drawer. "I was in too much of a hurry to pack neatly," Lisa answered. "Mama was breathing fire and I just wanted to get out of there."

"I know things didn't go well but she will cool off," Josie said calmly.

Lisa looked at her as if she had lost her mind.

"I mean, really, what choice does she have?" Josie said quickly after seeing Lisa's horrified expression. "The deed is done. You've moved out and life goes on. She'll get used to it and come to accept it."

Lisa had her doubts. "I don't know about that," Lisa said forebodingly. "You didn't hear what she said or see the look on her face. She was angrier than I've ever seen her."

Josie felt Lisa was exaggerating. "Come on, Lisa. Mama wouldn't think about killing her favorite. You're her darling little girl. That's why she's so upset over your move. Her baby is gone."

"I'm not so sure I agree with you. I intend to stay away from her house for a while. It may be safer for me that way," Lisa said as she put more shirts onto the bed.

"Girl, please! Mama is not going to hurt you, although I wouldn't put it past her to do something to teach you a lesson," Josie mused.

"Like what!" Lisa exclaimed. "Lock me in the basement for a week of torture?"

Josie laughed and walked over to hug Lisa and then pulled back.

"Don't be crazy! Mama's vengeful but she's not insane," Josie said warmly. "She probably wouldn't give you your mail or phone messages, something to aggravate you but not harm you. Everything will eventually work out. Just give it time. You'll see."

"I hope you're right, Josie. But I still have a bad feeling about this, a real bad feeling," Lisa said fearfully. For the first time in her life she was truly afraid of her mother.

Josie saw Lisa's fearful expression.

"Don't be afraid, Lisa. Everything's going to be okay. Just let some time pass," Josie said encouragingly.

Lisa sighed. Maybe they should change the subject.

"You know, I heard about your encounter with Rob the other night," Lisa said.

"Angie told you?" Josie asked.

"No. It was Sandra," Lisa responded.

"Whatever. I'm not sure they believed me," Josie said.

"I do," Lisa said.

"You do?" Josie asked in surprise.

"Yes, I do. And I've been thinking about what Rob said," Lisa said. "You know, when he said you were responsible for his death. I think he meant that you talked too much to Mama about your relationship."

"I don't know about that, Lisa," Josie disagreed. "Even if I did talk too much, Mama didn't kill Rob."

"I suppose she didn't but telling her your business didn't help. As a result, she was always in it. And Rob did mention your talking," Lisa persisted.

"Mama would have been in my business had I kept my mouth tight as a clam. That's just the way she is," Josie bemoaned.

Lisa was doubtful.

"Besides, Rob didn't say anything about Mama. You would think he would have if Mama had been involved in his death," Josie continued.

"I guess you're right. It was just a thought," Lisa said. "I guess I'm just weirded out because of my own problems with her."

Lisa sighed and look toward the window. She saw Josie's coat lying across the chair next to the window. She got up and picked up the coat to look more closely at it. Josie noticed her actions.

"That old coat has seen better days," Josie said with a laugh. "I need to have it cleaned and give it back to its owner."

Lisa looked sharply at her.

"This isn't your coat? You wear it all the time. Who does it belong to?" Lisa asked.

Josie laughed as she explained. "Sandra—" Josie began just as the telephone rang. "Hold on. Let me answer the phone."

Sandra, Lisa thought. What does she have to do with any of this? This whole mess was getting crazier by the minute. Josie was on the phone for a while and Lisa didn't give the coat any more thought. She didn't want not to get involved in Derek's case and she was sticking to her decision. When Josie finally got off the phone, they began talking of other things.

Duncan stood across the street from Josie's house staring at the light coming from the second story window.

It was her bedroom and she had not gone to sleep yet. It had only been ten days since his last visit with her but he couldn't seem too stay away. He had been watching Josie since the night he had made his demand of her. He knew where she went, who she saw and why. He knew of the changes that had occurred in her life. Her youngest sister had moved in with her. He could guess her reason for wanting Lisa living there but it did not perturb him. It was a minor nuisance but nothing that would keep him away from her. He didn't think anything could do that. He had finally admitted to himself that she had a pull on him, drawing him back to her. It wasn't the money that beckoned him to be in her presence. He soon realized that he didn't care about that. He wanted to be with her because he wanted to see her face, feel her creamy brown skin, hear her sultry voice, and caress her slim, enticing body. He wanted her but even more surprising is that he wanted her to want him. He couldn't stop remembering that night in her bedroom when he was laying the full length of her. He had felt the smooth contour of her body and it had triggered his need to possess her. It had taken every ounce of his willpower to refrain from making her his that very night. He didn't know how many more nights he could wait, hence he was standing in the shadows on her street watching her house...debating if he should go in or not. How he wished he could just storm the place and take what he wanted. It might be a bit barbaric but it would be oh so satisfying.

He sighed and tried to rein in his desires. He had been watching her house for a while now. He had seen

Lisa leave. He heard her tell Josie on the porch that she would be at her gig late and not to wait up for her. Good, he thought. Josie would be alone in the house. He had seen her sister Sandra pick up the kids. Apparently, she thought Josie needed a night to relax. He could help in that department if only Josie would let him. So the coast was clear if he chose to pay a visit. The opportunity was too perfect to let it slip away. He needed to see her. He would of course use the pretense of checking on her progress in securing the money. She must not know just yet that the money was not an issue. He saw the light in her window go out. She had retired for the night. He made sure no one was about before he left the shadow of a large parked truck. He ran across the street to take cover behind the huge oak tree in her front yard. Within seconds, he was on her porch, picked the lock, and slid inside. He gave a sigh of contentment. Josie was just a staircase away. He would soon see the object of his obsession.

It seemed like déjà vu as he mounted the steps two at a time, making sure he skipped the step that creaked. He silently eased down the darkened hallway until he reached the opened door of her room. She must have left it open so she would hear when Lisa got home. A concerned sister, he liked the trait. She was loving and caring. He needed that in his life. He wanted someone to care about him. Nobody had for a very long time. He had denied needing somebody since he was a wee lad. He was nine years old when he'd had to make it on his own. He'd quickly learned to connive, cheat, and steal if he wanted to survive in the slums of Scotland. God had blessed him with a quick and silky tongue. He rapidly learned to use it to his benefit. He had talked his way out of many sticky situations. He was sure he would need to engage in a little smooth talking in his pursuit of Josie. She was not going to welcome his suit. So be it. He would do whatever it took to win her favor. She was worth the extra effort. She was like a spring day in his beloved Scotland—sweet, pure, and lovely. She was a breath of fresh air. He needed Josie to breathe, to live. And he would not be denied.

He peeked into her bedroom. She was fast asleep. He quickly crossed the expanse between the door and her bed and threw himself on top of her. She instantly awoke and opened her mouth to scream. He clapped his hand over her lips preventing the howl that was sure to reverberate throughout the neighborhood. He looked in her beautiful hazel eyes and knew she recognized him.

"We really must stop meeting like this," Duncan drawled with a lazy smile. "It gives a strong, virile man like me interesting ideas."

She began to struggle against his hand as she punched him everywhere she could reach. She pummeled him until she grew tired. It was like beating a brick wall. It had no effect on him. She finally stopped.

"Are you finished now? I hope you've gotten it all out of your system," he murmured. "I will happily remove my hand when I am certain you will not scream the house down. Think of your sister and your children. Oh, but they are not here. You are alone…with me."

Her hazel eyes had darkened to a simmering charcoal. Although it wasn't in her nature to hate, she looked at him with as much loathing as she could muster. She was furious and he knew it but it didn't seem to bother him.

"All done?" he asked casually.

She nodded her head affirmatively. He slowly removed his hand. She opened her mouth to scream. He quickly covered it again.

"Really, Josie. I only want to talk to you, just a friendly conversation. You can't really object to that, can you?" he questioned. "Let's try this again." He removed his hand. Josie remained quiet. "Good," he said with a smile.

Josie almost imagined that his smile was tender but knew it couldn't be so. He was a ruthless man who would do anything to get what he wanted, and he wanted money that she didn't have. But she still had more time. So why was he here? To torment her? She was doing enough of that herself, she didn't need him to do so as well. He shifted and she became aware of the fact that he had not removed his long, muscular frame from her body, and deep inside a tiny voice was telling her that she didn't want him to. It was crazy but she grudgingly admitted that it was true. She instinctively knew that he was not going to harm her. She knew that she was safe with him and she did not want to lose the protective and sensuous feeling that his body gave her.

Little did she know that Duncan was having similar feelings of his own. She felt so damn good, he thought. He knew he was too heavy for her but he couldn't bring himself to ease off of her. It felt like he belonged there and those feelings hadn't stirred in his breast since he was a wee lad. Tender thoughts of home and hearth no longer existed in his world. She moved slightly and it ignited a flame deep within him that he wasn't sure he could extinguish. He wasn't certain if he wanted to put it out. He looked down at her beautiful face. Her skin was creamy milk chocolate; so soft and smooth. His mouth was resting just beneath her ear. A slight turn of his head and he would be able to kiss and caress that tempting spot. But he knew if he kissed her neck it would be nearly impossible for him not to satisfy his raging appetite. He felt her move her hand against the back of his neck. Her slender fingers played with his thick, shoulder length, black hair. It was almost his undoing. He abruptly sat up, removing his large body from her small contour. He took several deep breaths to restore his composure.

"Let's talk business, shall we?" he said sharply.

Josie was slightly disconcerted. Somehow she felt bereft without the pressure of his body against hers. She quickly lowered her eyes so he wouldn't see the abandonment she was feeling. She shouldn't be having these feelings anyway. She berated herself for feeling anything but anger and contempt for him. He was threatening to do her bodily harm if she didn't come up with the money. She should detest him, not want him to kiss her. She shook her head to clear it and then looked at him with determined resolve. She was not going to let him intimidate her. She still had more time to get the money. She was not going to allow him to browbeat her about it.

"Why are you here?" she looked him straight in the eye. Her tone was unyielding.

Duncan saw the strength of mind in her clear, hazel eyes. She was not going to let him bully her. His lips formed a crooked smile. This was going to be fun. He casually crossed his legs and leaned back on his elbows on the bed.

"I'm here for a status report," he said casually. "I have much interest in your progress."

What progress, she thought. She had not secured nearly enough of the money that Rob owed him. And she knew she wasn't going to. She had no way of raising that kind of money. But she continued to present a brave face.

"I'll have your money," what a crock she thought. "I just require the full three weeks you promised me."

Duncan wanted this game to continue much longer.

"I tell you what, being that I am a fair man and I know this matter must be causing undue stress," he said with concern. "So I will extend your time another six weeks. That will be of much help. Yes?"

Another six weeks! Josie was almost giddy with relief. She knew she would be able to find a way out of this mess in that amount of time. "Yes, that will help," she managed to say soberly.

"Good. It will give us more time to get to know one another," Duncan smiled devilishly.

What was he talking about? she thought. They didn't need to know each other anymore than they did already. She didn't want to know him better. It pained her to admit it but she just didn't trust herself to be around him. Her traitorous body had a mind of its own when it came to him. He was just too darn handsome and sexy for her own peace of mind. Having him around more often was a bad idea; a very bad idea.

Duncan saw the war going on in her head. He decided to press his suit.

"We will have dinner tomorrow night. We will become friends. Yes?"

No! We cannot become friends. He's acting as though he's not holding an ax over her neck. Although she intuitively knew that he would not harm her, they still could not be friends...they just couldn't! Somehow she had to convince him that they would be better off as just associates and nothing more. But Lord! She was drawn to what the 'more' suggested.

"No. I think we should leave things as they are. I feel it would be best," she said firmly.

"Why?" he asked with much interest.

Why? Well, she certainly couldn't tell him the real reason. She had to think fast.

"It's not a good idea to mix business with pleasure."

She groaned as he grinned at her. She couldn't believe those words had come out of her mouth. So much for thinking on her feet. He shifted on the bed and rested his head on her legs.

"It's been my experience that mixing a little enjoyment with business can render ideal results," he smiled slowly.

She attempted to jostle her legs to remove his head from her lap but to no avail. He was too heavy. And his weight was also comfortable. She groaned as sparks of desire shot up her legs. The situation was so danger-ous. She knew she should pull her legs away and tuck them beneath her but she couldn't. The pressure of his head on her legs felt too good. It felt right for him to be relaxed against her. He was watching her, expecting an answer. She wanted to agree to dinner for the next day but knew that she shouldn't. Suddenly, they heard a door close. He was off the bed in an instant, his hand gripping the hilt of his dagger.

"Josie! I'm home!" Lisa called up the stairs.

"She's home early," Duncan said calmly.

Josie could only nod. She had no idea as to why Lisa was home so soon. Duncan stood with his legs slightly apart and his free hand relaxed at his side. They heard Lisa traipsing up the steps and walking down the hall. Lisa entered Josie's room and promptly screamed. Josie understood Lisa's reaction. As handsome as Duncan was, he was still a frightful sight until you got used to him. His huge muscular breadth along with his tower-ing height made him appear formidable in the extreme. She could only imagine the terror Lisa must be feel-ing as she looked at him. Duncan approached Lisa, his hand extended in greeting. Lisa turned to run but Duncan was too fast for her. He caught her arm and pulled her against him. Lisa was a prisoner in his arms. Irrationally, Josie actually envied her.

"Let me go," Lisa yelled.

Josie shook her head and scrambled out of bed and moved to Lisa's side. She held Lisa's other arm.

"Let her go, Duncan. Please." Her hazel eyes pleaded for him to relent.

Duncan knew he could deny her nothing. He had no intention of harming Lisa but he had to restrain her. He slowly released Lisa's arm. She moved immediately away from him as she chaffed her arm. She stared at him mutinously.

"Who is he? And why is he in your bedroom?" Lisa demanded of Josie.

"Sweetie, it's okay. He's okay," Josie said soothingly. "This is Duncan—" She stopped as she realized she didn't know his last name. She looked at him in askance.

Duncan seldom revealed his last name. In his line of work, it was better if it were not known.

"Duncan will suffice," he replied cordially.

Josie looked at him with doubt but went on with his introduction to Lisa.

"This is Duncan. He's a…um…an acquaintance of Rob's."

"And you're entertaining him in your bedroom?" Lisa was suspicious. She looked at the two of them. Something wasn't adding up.

"No! It's not what you think," Josie exclaimed.

"Too bad," Duncan murmured.

Josie shot him a look of annoyance. Duncan just grinned.

"Then what is it?" Lisa demanded.

Josie searched her mind for a plausible answer. She certainly couldn't give her the real explanation.

"It's…well, actually…it's—"

"A bit of business. But Josie and I can certainly continue our talk tomorrow at supper," Duncan intervened smoothly.

"Supper? Tomorrow?" Lisa was shocked.

"Guess who's coming to dinner?" Duncan quipped with raised eyebrows.

"Perhaps tomorrow isn't—" Josie's voice trailed off when her eyes met his. She knew he would be there regardless of any excuses she might voice. His eyes were glittering spheres of amber steel, hard and unrelenting. Trying to deny him what he wanted was futile.

Lisa was thoroughly confused. What was going on here? Obviously Josie knew more than she was saying but suddenly she was incapable of speech.

Duncan moved to the door and paused. "Until tomorrow, dear ladies," he said.

He left so quickly and silently that one would almost wonder if he had ever been there at all. But one look at Josie and that question was answered in spades. Josie moved to plop onto the bed. She looked as though the weight of the world was on her shoulders. Lisa went to sit bed beside her. She clasped Josie's folded hands which lay on her lap.

"Talk to me, Josie," Lisa said quietly. "What's going on?"

Josie took a deep breath and turned to look at Lisa. Her erratic emotions had drained her. She didn't know what to do. She had to confide in somebody. She no longer wanted to be in this all by herself. She began to tell Lisa the entire story.

CHAPTER 10

Millie entered her bedroom and moved to her dresser. She stood there looking at her face in the mirror. She saw a few fine lines etching her face and there were dark shadows under her clear gray eyes, but the skin was tight and smooth. There were no wrinkles marring the downy complexion. She had aged very well. She didn't look her fifty-eight years. Millie continued looking at the visage until it began to fade into another Millie of a youthful year. She patted her hair into place and set a smart black hat with a red feather tucked into the band onto her head. She adjusted it slightly to one side and smiled broadly at her appearance. She looked good. Even Leon would have to admit that she looked real nice. She heard a creak. She saw the door open in the reflection of the mirror. Leon stumbled into the room. Millie turned to face him grinning widely.

"I'm ready! How do I look?" Millie asked gaily.

Leon stumbled to the armchair and sat down. He slouched in the chair. He slurred his words as he spoke. "Ready for what?" he asked drunkenly.

"We're going to church," Millie slowly replied. She tried to remain happy. "You said we could go to church this Sunday. How do I look?"

"How are you 'pose to look? You look like you always look…like an old hag. What's that thing you have on that straw you call hair?" Leon laughed at his cruel joke.

The smile faded from Millie's face. She nervously touched her hat. "It's my new hat. I really like it. Don't you, Leon?" Millie queried.

"Naw. It was a waste of money. Shoulda used that money to buy me some food. I'm hungry," he complained.

"We're supposed to go to church, Leon. Hurry and get dressed so we won't be late," she coaxed him gently.

"I ain't going to no church and neither are you. You needs to make me somethin' to eat. I told you I's hungry," he said angrily.

"You've been out all night with that slut at the club, haven't you?" Millie said disgustedly.

"What iffin' I have? It ain't yo business," he snapped.

"It's every bit of my business and I'm not going to put up with it anymore," she said darkly.

"Like you can change it," he laughed. "Git on out of here and git my breakfast."

"Git your own damned breakfast," Millie muttered as she turned to face the dresser.

"What the hell did you say?" Leon shouted.

"No more. No more." She spoke as if she were talking to herself.

"What you blatherin about? And take that hat off. You look stupid in it. It should be worn by a pretty woman, not you," he said meanly.

Millie slowly removed the hat and opened the top drawer of the dresser. She laid the hat gently inside the drawer then moved her hands beneath the blouses that were neatly folded on top. She curled her fingers around a cold steel handle. She looked at Leon through the mirror and muttered. "No more."

The memory faded as Millie's older face materialized in the mirror. She opened the drawer of the old wooden dresser and pulled out the black hat with the red feather. Then she reached under the folded blouses and pulled out an old friend. She caressed the wood and metal handle.

"Hi, Mama!"

Angie and Sandra spoke simultaneously as they entered the room. Millie quickly put the hat and old friend back into the drawer and slammed it shut. She turned around to face her daughters.

"What are you doing here?" Millie asked sharply.

"We just came over for a visit," Sandra said. "We haven't heard from you so we thought we would come by."

"Oh! Well, come into the kitchen and I'll get you some iced tea," Millie said hurriedly.

She bustled out of the room and Sandra followed. Angie stayed behind and moved over to the dresser. Angie thought that Millie had acted strangely when they entered the room. Millie had hurriedly closed the dresser drawer as if she were hiding something. What was it? Angie looked over her shoulder to be sure no one was coming then she quietly opened the drawer. She saw a hat lying on top of some clothing. She picked it up and put it on. She smiled at her reflection.

"It's cute," she murmured.

She took it off and replaced it. She was about to close the drawer when her fingers touched something lying against the front inside panel of the drawer. It was hard and cold. Angie tried to get a firm grip on the object. She pulled it out.

"Oh my God!" She exclaimed softly.

She quickly removed her scarf from her neck and wrapped the object in it. She then slipped it into her bag. It was a good thing that she carried large purses. She zipped her bag and left the room. She did not realize that Millie had been peeping through the window that faced the back garden.

Angie entered the kitchen.

"I've just remembered an appointment that I have," Angie said in a rush. "It completely slipped my mind until now. I'll be late if I don't hurry."

"We just got here. And where have you been?" Sandra asked in exasperation.

"In the bathroom," Angie improvised.

Millie came through the back door holding a pitcher of tea. "I've been brewing this out in the sun all morning," Millie said. "It should be ready by now. Angie, get the glasses."

"Oh Mama, I'm sorry but we can't stay," Angie said hurriedly. "We have an appointment that we forgot all about." She hoped that the use of "we" would make the excuse sound more feasible.

"What appointment?" Millie stared at her.

Angie pulled Sandra from the chair so forcefully that Sandra stumbled.

"There's someone that we have to meet." Angie explained quickly.

"We do?" Sandra asked baffled as Angie ushered her out of the room.

"See you soon, Mama!" Angie called as she pushed Sandra toward the front door. Angie grabbed their coats and opened the door, practically thrusting Sandra through it. She closed the door and gave Sandra her coat.

"What's wrong with you? What was all that about?" Sandra demanded.

"I've got to go see Derek. I'll drop you off at home. Come on," Angie said and ran down the steps and crossed the lawn to the car.

"I don't understand," Sandra exclaimed as she hurried to the car.

"There's no time to explain. Just come on," Angie replied.

They got into the car and drove off. Millie angrily watched them leave through the front window.

Derek was sitting at his desk twirling a pencil. He suddenly broke it.

"Breaking a pencil usually indicates frustration," Sam said as he sat on the corner of Derek's desk.

"That describes my mood," Derek said irritably. He threw the broken piece onto his desk. "I'm getting absolutely nowhere in Rob's case, or the cold cases."

"We'll get a break soon," Sam said.

Derek looked at him in annoyance.

"Pardon the pun." Sam laughed.

"You know, Sam, there are days when I wish I had become an accountant," Derek said as he leaned back in his chair and closed his eyes.

"And you wouldn't have lasted a week. You would have been bored out of your mind," Sam smirked as he folded his arms across his stomach.

"You're right," Derek grimaced and opened his eyes. "And I'm horrible with math. But knowing this does not help solve this case. I need a lead…a strong one and I don't have it."

"Well, maybe you're about to get one. Here's comes your darling wife. Looks like she's on a mission," Sam pointed to Angie marching determinedly down the hall.

Derek wasn't sure if he were happy or afraid to see his wife. She looked like she was ready to explode. Derek stood up as she reached his desk. Extending his arms to hug her, he stopped short as she shoved her scarf against his chest.

"Get this tested, Derek. Right away," Angie demanded.

Derek grasped the bundle.

"Your scarf?"

"No! It's what's in the scarf that needs to be analyzed," she said with impatience. She noticed Sam. "Hi, Sam."

"Hey, Angie," Sam replied. He watched Derek with interest as he unwrapped the scarf.

Sam whistled as he saw the wicked-looking dagger.

"This isn't Josie's. Where did you get this and whose is it?" Derek asked.

Angie sighed and looked as if she were ready to collapse. Derek quickly ushered her into the chair by his desk.

"Baby, are you all right? Have some water," Derek said in concern.

Sam poured a steroid cup of water from the pitcher on the desk. He handed it to Angie. She took a large swallow of water. Derek squatted in front of her and gently caressed her cheek. Worry was etched in his face.

"I'm okay," she said shakily. "I was just so anxious to see you. I couldn't get here soon enough."

"Tell me where you got this," Derek said quietly.

Angie took a deep breath. "It belongs to Mama," Angie said. "I found it tucked away in her dresser drawer."

Derek was alarmed. "You went snooping around in your mother's bedroom? Angie! You could have been caught."

"But I wasn't. And it's not as though I intended to rummage through her things. The opportunity presented itself and I took advantage of it," Angie said. She proceeded to recount her visit to her mother's house.

Sam opened the folder that was lying on the corner of Derek's desk. He took out the drawing of the weapon that was thought to be the murder weapon in Richard and Patrick's case. He handed the drawing to Derek.

"Compare it," Sam said grimly.

Derek moved to sit in his chair and carefully used the scarf to place the knife next to the drawing.

"It's a close match if not exact," Sam said. "We've been looking for a traditional kitchen knife when maybe we should have been looking for a dagger."

"The notes in the files indicated the murder weapon for the household cooking utensil. The detectives may have been wrong in their assessment of the murder weapon," Sam said thoughtfully.

"We still don't know if this is the murder weapon," Derek said.

"The preliminary match is a good one," Sam replied.

"We still need to send it to forensics for testing," Derek murmured. He looked at Angie and said. "Are you sure Mama didn't see you take this?"

Angela hesitated then said.

"I'm sure. I mean, I didn't see her around when I took it. She couldn't have seen me."

"We may have been focusing on the wrong kind of blade," Derek said thoughtfully.

"The information in the files called it a kitchen knife. We can't be faulted for going with that data," Sam objected.

"But we can be faulted for not looking at all possibilities. We're supposed to think out of the box when all else fails," Derek argued.

"But Millie? She has no motive," Sam said.

"Maybe she does," Derek began thinking about his talk with Millie at her birthday party. He told them about the incident.

"You can't take a conversation out of context and say Mama had a motive to kill." Angie was appalled.

"If you didn't have a suspicion that Mama could be a suspect, why did you bring me the dagger?" Derek challenged her.

Angela's indignation seeped out of her. She had no answer.

"I'm sorry, baby, but I have to follow this through," Derek said kindly. He looked at Sam. "We need Josie's coat. I have a hunch there's a link between the coat and the dagger."

"But the dagger belongs to Mama," Angie said perplexed.

"I know. But there must be an explanation," Derek said reasonably.

"Now I have to get the coat and then my good deed for you will be done," Angie smiled at Derek.

"No. You've done enough," Derek said abruptly. "We've had this discussion, Angie. You are not doing anything. It's enough that you took a chance in bringing me this dagger."

"Honey—"

"No, Angie. It's settled. Sam and I will take it from here," Derek stated flatly.

"Why don't I go over to see Lisa and nose around a bit," Sam suggested. "If I see the coat I'll think of a reason to secure it."

A knowing look crossed Angie's face and she smiled. Sam ducked his head and quickly rose from his desk. He took his coat from the nearby rack and put it on.

"You'll need a warrant," Derek said. "I'll call the courthouse for one and you can stop by to get it on your way to Josie's house."

"All right. I'll be back in a few," he said as he rushed to the elevator before anyone could say anything.

"I hope his trip proves fruitful in more ways than one," Derek said.

Angie smiled and left her seat to sit on Derek's lap. She wrapped her arms around his neck.

"I think he'll get to first base," She smiled.

"And will I? I know very well how much you dislike not getting your way," he grinned.

"Well, you did throw me out before I could get to first base." she pouted.

"That I did. I couldn't help it. I love you too much." He kissed her neck. "But the question remains, will I score when I get home tonight?"

"You'll see when you come home," she smiled as she returned his gesture with a kiss on his neck.

"I'll be home early," he promised.

Angie chuckled and rose from his lap.

"I foresee the seventh inning stretch being very interesting," she said saucily.

She turned and walked to the elevator. Derek grinned as he picked up the phone to call the courthouse.

Lisa hurried to the door to answer the bell. She opened the door and looked at her visitor in exasperation.

"What are you doing here?" Lisa blurted out rudely. Recent events had made her unnaturally testy.

Sam ignored Lisa's bad temper and walked into the house.

"I didn't invite you in," she said indignantly.

"I need to talk to you. Is Josie here?" Sam asked as he looked at Lisa's outraged but lovely face. He thought she was gorgeous when she was mad.

Lisa closed the door. "No but she should be back soon," she said sullenly as she closed the door. She remembered her manners and asked. "Can I take your coat?"

"Sure." He took off his coat and she hung it on the coat rack in the hall.

"Come into the living room and tell me why you're here," she said as she led the way into the room.

She sat on the sofa and he sat next to her. She looked at him expectantly. He decided he may as well dive in.

"There's no sense in beating around the bush. We need need Josie's coat. It's crucial. I have a warrant to search the house for it," he said quickly.

Lisa looked at him sadly.

"So, it's come to this? I was hoping that Derek would be able to find another way," she sighed.

"We don't have a choice, Lisa. We need it to prove the case one way or another," Sam said gently.

"So Derek sent you to be the bad guy," Lisa smiled ruefully.

"I was none too eager about the prospect of facing you but I had to come," Sam said earnestly.

"I'll never believe that Josie is guilty," Lisa said vehemently.

"Josie's coat doesn't necessarily target her," Sam said.

Lisa shook her head in confusion. "What do you mean? You have another suspect? Who?" she demanded.

Lisa was quick. That's one of the things that he liked about her. There were a lot of things he liked about her. She was pretty, witty, humorous. She could sing, dance, and she loved to laugh. She was just about the perfect girl. He just had to figure out a way to make her his girl.

"Earth to Sam! Are you with me?" Lisa snapped her fingers.

"Oh sorry! I was thinking," he explained.

"About telling me who the new suspect is?" Lisa suggested.

"No, I can't. You will have to trust me," he said with a smile.

She didn't respond for a moment. Then she looked him straight in his honey-brown eyes.

"Can I trust you, Sam?" Lisa asked earnestly.

"Yes. You can trust me with your life," he solemnly replied. He meant every word of what he had just said.

"All right. I don't know what this is all about but I'm going to trust that you have good reason for wanting it. And you'd better tell me everything when it's all over," she sighed.

"I promise," he pledged.

She stood up and walked into the hall. She removed Josie's coat from the hook and took it back into the room.

"It was fairly warm this morning when she left house so she didn't wear it," Lisa explained. "I still don't understand why you need it. It's not even hers," she said.

Sam's ears perked up. "What do you mean it's not hers?" he questioned.

"She told me it belonged to Sandra," Lisa said off-handedly.

"How long has she had it?" Sam questioned.

"It's been a while, I guess," she said with a shrug. "The phone rang when we were talking about it. She stopped to answer the phone and we never finished our conversation. I'm sure Josie intended to give it back to

Sandra, but she hasn't had the money to replace it with a new one."

Sam stood up and took the coat from her.

"This throws a twist into things," he mumbled.

"What did you say?" Lisa questioned curiously

"Uhh, nothing," Sam said hurriedly.

Lisa looked at him shrewdly. "It's something but you're not going to tell me, are you?" Lisa said sagely.

He smiled at her crookedly. "No." He put his hands on her shoulders and continued. "You know I can't. But soon."

"Waiting is not my strong suit," she mumbled.

He laughed. "Let me make it up to you by buying you dinner," he said.

Lisa opened and shut her mouth two times. She was completely taken off guard. He saw her indecision and pressed his suit.

"Have dinner with me, Lisa. I promise you won't regret it."

She looked at him as if seeing him for the first time. She liked what she saw. He was tall, very well built, and handsome. Why she hadn't given him a second look, she didn't know. But there was no time like the present. She gave him a smile that lit up her face.

"I would love to," she responded.

He grinned and pulled her in for a hug. "Great. I'll pick you up tonight at seven," he said.

She pulled out of his arms.

"Uhh, no. Tonight isn't good," she said nervously. "Tomorrow would be better," she said quickly. Duncan would be here tonight and she didn't want the two of them to meet.

"Tomorrow it is. I'll see you then," he said.

He adjusted the coat on his arm and followed her to the door.

"I'll tell Josie that the police department confiscated her coat. She's going to freak out when she learns that you are considering her as a suspect," Lisa said.

"There are elements involved that you don't know anything about, Lisa. Try not to worry," Sam sighed.

"Easier said than done," Lisa grimaced.

"It's going to be alright. Trust me," Sam encouraged.

"I'll try," she smiled wanly.

"I'll give it back to you as soon as possible," Sam said as he looked into her upturned face. Her eyes were bright with anticipation. "Until tomorrow."

He quickly left the house. Lisa stood in the door and watched him get in his car and drive off. She slowly closed the door and thought she could barely wait for tomorrow to arrive.

CHAPTER 11

Jimmy was sitting at his desk leaning back in his chair reading a legal brief. He looked up when his door open. A wide grin spread across his face.

"Sandra. What brings you to my office," he stood and crossed the small office to hug her.

"Hi, baby. I just wanted to see you," she said softly. "I needed to see you."

He pulled back from her to read her somber expression. Leading her to a green-cushioned, short-backed armchair, he seated her and then sat on the corner of his cluttered desk.

"What's wrong? You seem upset," he said.

"I don't know exactly. It's just that nothing seems as it should. Angie is acting suspiciously. She and I were at Mama's house this morning and suddenly she had to leave. She bolted us out there as if the house was on fire. But she wouldn't answer any questions when I asked her about it. Lisa moved out of Mama's place very abruptly. Josie is hiding secrets and Mama looks as though she's ready to murder somebody," Sandra exclaimed. "Nobody is acting normally."

"Honey, do you think you could be overreacting?" he questioned.

"No. Something is off with everybody. It's not my imagination," she answered certainly.

"Okay. What do you think it could be?" he asked.

"I don't know for sure. But nothing has been quite the same since Robert died," she murmured.

"And Derek started looking into the deaths of Patrick and Richard. I know he's investigating Rob's death but why would he start poking around in Richard and Patrick's cases. Does he think there's a connection?" Jimmy speculated.

"I didn't know he was investigating Richard and Patrick's deaths," Sandra said in surprise.

"I just kind of put two and two together from a few things I overheard Derek saying to Sam at Josie's a few weeks ago. They didn't realize I had heard them and I didn't broach the subject with them," he said.

"Maybe he's found a link between the three cases but that wouldn't explain my sisters' strange behavior," she mulled.

"Well, your sisters act a little strange anyway," he chuckled. "It's normal behavior for them."

"This is nothing to joke about, Jimmy," she reproached him.

"Well, worrying about it is not going to give us any answers. I'm sure it will all work itself out one way or another," he said as he rose from his perch on the desk and assisted her to stand. "Come on. What I have to do here can wait until tomorrow. Let's go home. I have an intense need to be with my wife and kids."

Sandra smiled at him. "I have that same desire," she said softly.

They walked to the door. He switched off the lights as they exited the office.

Millie rummaged through her dresser drawer searching desperately for the dagger. It wasn't there. She thought that she had seen Angie take it but she hadn't been sure. Now she was. She had to rectify the matter. She moved to her rocking chair by the window and sat down. She looked out the window and saw birds flying toward their resting place for the night. The sky was darkening and the wind was rising. Dogs barked in the distance and police sirens shrilled. Car doors slammed shut as her neighbors hurried into their homes. Millie gently rocked as she listened to the sounds of the night and thought about what had to be done. Her husband had left her alone. Three of her four daughters had married and left her alone. Now, her baby, Lisa, was gone doing who knows what just to sing a song. She had that same bad seed that had ruined Bethelee. Well, they fixed Bethelee and she would fix Lisa too. It would be for the best.

She was deserted yet again. She had been by herself for most of her life. She should be used to it but she wasn't. She didn't like it. It wasn't right to live all alone. Why couldn't people just live together without leaving each other? It seemed that people always forced her to be solitary. Well, she refused to accept it. Something had to be done. The bare floor creaked where Millie rocked unceasingly. She stared at the starless, cloudy sky as she continued to think deep into the night.

Josie entered through her front door and closed it with a great sigh. She leaned against the door and closed her eyes. She thought about what a hectic, nerve-racking morning it had been. Kimberly couldn't find anything to her liking to wear to school and her book bag had mysteriously disappeared into thin air. Too bad Kimberly's science report was in it and it was due today. While she was searching for the backpack, little Robbie decided to wake and scream the neighbors awake. Thank goodness Lisa had taken care of Robbie and she had finally located the elusive backpack in the mud room where Kim had thoughtlessly dropped it the day before. Of course she had no memory of having done so. Kim finally found something to wear to her satisfaction and after a quick breakfast Josie carted her off to the bus stop and put her on the school bus. She opened her eyes to see Lisa sitting on the steps staring at her. Drat! This day only promised to get worse.

"What now?" Josie demanded. She didn't know if she could handle another crisis.

"Duncan," Lisa said flatly.

Josie pushed away from the door and walked down the hall.

"I need a cup of coffee," Josie said.

Lisa rose from the steps and followed her doggedly.

"Josie, we have to talk about this. I didn't sleep at all last night," she said insistently.

"Not before I have my cup of coffee, Lisa," Josie said. "The topic of my tormentor will have to wait."

In the kitchen, Josie poured herself a mug of coffee and sat at the table. She proceeded to lace her beverage with sugar and cream. Lisa sat down at the table.

"Seriously, Josie. We have to figure out what we're going to do," Lisa began. "That highwayman means business."

"He won't harm us," Josie murmured before taking a sip of her coffee.

"How do you know? He looks like he could cheerfully snap your neck within the time it takes you to blink," Lisa argued.

"I just know. Duncan won't harm us. He only wants his money," Josie responded reasonably.

Lisa looked at her in shock. She thought that Josie had finally lost it. Her usual practicality and common sense had gone visiting due to all of the stress and strain she'd been under. But, holy crap, she had to snap out of it. This wasn't the time for her to become a loony tune.

"Josie! You're not thinking clearly, for if you were, you would realize that Duncan is a dangerous character. We need to call the police," Lisa stated firmly.

Josie slammed her mug down on the table.

"No. Under no circumstances will we involve the police. Duncan has not done anything but ask for the money that he is owed. That is not criminal," Josie forcefully.

"It is when he expects to get paid by someone he didn't strike the deal with. You didn't make the agreement with him. Rob did. And he's dead. Just as the deal should be. Dead. Dead. Dead," Lisa emphasized.

"Well, that isn't the case. So we will just have to deal with it," Josie said resolutely.

"How?" Lisa demanded incredulously. She could not believe that Josie was not upset about what was happening. How could she be so calm? "How can you sit there and act like all is well when it isn't?"

"It's just a feeling I have," Josie said.

Lisa sat back in her chair and rolled her eyes.

"And don't look at me like that. I know it sounds ridiculous but I just have this unshakable, peaceful feeling that everything will be all right. Don't ask me how because I don't know. But I am going to trust my gut," Josie said decisively.

"Until Duncan rips it out of you," Lisa retorted.

"That won't happen," Josie stated confidently.

"Well, I hope your gut is right or else we're sunk," Lisa said irritably.

The doorbell rang. They looked at each other in alarm.

"Duncan! It's too early for him to be here," Lisa exclaimed.

The bell rang twice more insistently.

"Try to relax. It may not be him," Josie said as she stood and walked down the hall. Lisa followed closely behind her.

Derek hung up the phone, tension lines etched in his forehead. The memory that had prompted that phone call was very disturbing with potentially threatening ramifications. Derek had finally remembered the vague memory that had been plaguing him and the implication was extremely unsettling. They had all been at Millie's for Sunday dinner and Millie had graciously offered her coat to Sandra, who was in need of a heavier coat for the winter. Sandra accepted gratefully and as she swung the coat over her shoulders, Derek saw the torn hem. He hadn't thought anything of it at the time. That wasn't the case now. The information he had garnered from his conversation with Sandra had shed an unsavory light on his case. He didn't like the picture that the completed puzzle presented but he had to deal with it all the same. He picked up the forensic reports that had come back on Josie's coat and Mama's dagger. He had put a rush on the analytical team to process the items as quickly as possible. Now that he had the reports, he almost wished that he had never started this investigation. He read the findings again for what seemed like the hundredth time. He couldn't deny the implication.

He stood and was hurriedly donning his coat when Sam arrived at his desk.

"Where are you rushing off to?" Sam asked in surprise.

"I've got to take care of something," Derek mumbled.

It didn't escape Sam's notice when Derek took his gun out of the drawer and slid it into its holster.

"I'll go with you," Sam said.

"No. That's not necessary," Derek muttered.

"I think it is. Derek, you know me. Whatever it is, you can trust me. Let me go with you," Sam urged.

"I said no," Derek snapped. He then looked at Sam's expression of confusion. He sighed and said. "Look, I promise to call in. I just need to do this alone. We cool?"

"Yeah. Okay," Sam said reluctantly. "Be sure to call in."

"I will," Derek said as he rapidly walked to the elevator.

Sam watched him enter the elevator then glanced over to his desk. He saw two folders laying there. He reached over and picked up one of the folders. After reading the reports inside, he reached for the phone and dialed.

Angie was vacuuming her living room when she heard someone pounding on the door. She turned off the vacuum and went to the door. Looking through the peephole, she saw who it was and opened the door.

"We've got to talk," the visitor said.

"And good morning to you too," Angie said sardonically as she closed the door.

"I'm serious, Angie. I'm worried, frustrated, and scared. You know something and you've got to tell me what it is," Sandra said in a rush.

"Come on. Sit down. I'll go make us some tea," Angie said.

Sandra sat down on the sofa.

"I don't want any tea. I want answers," Sandra grumbled.

"You need it to calm your nerves," Angie called to her as she went into the kitchen.

Sandra sat back on the sofa and rubbed her forehead. The morning's events had disturbed her. She needed answers and she instinctively knew that Angie could supply them. After a few more minutes, Angie came back carrying two mugs of hot tea. She handed a cup to Sandra.

"I made it just the way you like it," Angie smiled.

Sandra took the cup and sipped from it.

"You're right. The tea is helping but I still need answers," Sandra said.

"All right. I will give you as many answers as I can," Angie said. She knew she would not hold back from telling Sandra the entire story. Sandra was her sister and they didn't keep secrets from one another for very long. They were too close.

"When did Derek start investigating Richard and Patrick's murders?" Sandra clear grey eyes watched her intently.

"How did you know?" Angie asked.

"Jimmy told me," Sandra answered.

Angie was surprised.

"How did Jimmy—"

"Oh never mind about Jimmy, Angie," Sandra said in exasperation. "Tell me what's going on. I know you know. So spill it."

Angie took a deep breath. "Okay, here's the story," Angie began. Angie related the entire story.

"Oh my God! Now it all makes sense. Kind of," Sandra said as she put her cup on the table.

"What do you mean?" Angie questioned.

"Well, Derek called me this morning and asked me about my coat," Sandra said confusedly.

"Your coat? Are you sure it wasn't about Josie's coat?" Angie was baffled.

"That isn't what he asked me about. He was intent—" Sandra was cut off by the ring of the doorbell.

"Oh, who could that be?" Angie said as she rose to answer the door.

Angie opened the door and was shocked.

"Aunt Bethelee," she cried out.

Sandra quickly joined Angie at the door.

"Angie, hello, my dear," Bethelee looked at Sandra and greeted her. "Sandra, how are you? May I come in?"

Angie and Sandra stepped back.

"Of course. Come in," Angie invited.

Bethelee untied the woolen scarf she wore around her neck and looked around.

"Here, let me take your coat," Angie said.

Bethelee removed her coat and gave it to Angie.

"Please, sit, Aunt Bethelee," Sandra gestured to the armchair adjacent to the sofa.

"Thank you," Bethelee said as she lowered her slight, petite frame into the chair.

Angie looked at Bethelee closely as she moved to the closet to hang up her fur-accented black leather coat. Her dress and shoes looked new and expensive. Her matching earrings and necklace looked like authentic emeralds and even her untrained eye could see that the rock on her manicured finger was surely a diamond. Obviously, Aunt Bethelee had done well for herself. She must be in her early sixties but she looked like she was barely in her forties. She had aged well. Her skin was smooth and appeared soft to the touch.

"This is such a nice house, Angie. You and Derek have done well," Bethelee smiled.

"Thank you. We're far from having arrived but we're doing okay. We want to start a family soon," Angie said.

Bethelee smiled sadly. "Little ones running about will be good. Every house needs the sound of children in it," Bethelee said softly.

"I would love to meet your children, Aunt Bethelee. They're my cousins, after all," Angie said as she sat on the sofa next to Sandra.

"I don't have any children," Bethelee's face hardened.

"I'm sorry. I just assumed. I shouldn't have," Angie said quietly.

"It's all right. It was God's will...somewhat," Bethelee responded.

Sandra and Angie were nonplussed at Bethelee's answer.

"We're so glad you're here, Aunt Bethelee. It's been so long since we've seen you," Sandra said.

"Yes, it has been many years. I've lived and performed in Europe for most of my life. But I've always kept up with you all," Bethelee said.

"Kept up with us? But you haven't been around since we were children," Angie said mystified.

"But I know about every milestone in your lives all the same. I was aware of when you married, Sandra, both times. And your wedding as well, Angie. I know about Josie and Lisa too," Bethelee said softly. "How is Josie holding up? Her loss must be very difficult for her."

"She's doing as well as can be expected," Sandra responded.

So, Aunt Bethelee really was keeping up with the events in their lives, Angie thought. It was nice to know someone was watching over you but it felt a little peculiar as well. To have a virtual stranger spying on you was unnerving.

"You were watching over us even though you weren't here. Why didn't you come around? We all wondered about you," Angie said.

"There were reasons, child. Reasons you know nothing about," Bethelee said emotionally.

"But you're here now. Why?" Sandra asked.

"Lisa," Bethelee said simply. "I'm here for Lisa."

"Lisa? I don't understand," Angie said full of perplexity.

"You will," Bethelee began telling the tale. "It all started long before you were born."

The heavy, murky clouds finally opened and the snow began to fall. It fell heavily for hours. Millie looked out her kitchen window and felt that the weather matched her mood. But eventually it would stop snowing and when she was done preparing her remedy, her problems would stop as well. She turned back to the table and poured the liquid mixture from the glass funnel into a small medicine bottle. She screwed the top on securely and stared at the filled bottle. She set the bottle on the table and reached for the syringe that was lying on a paper towel. She wrapped the towel tightly around the syringe and put both the small bottle and syringe in a small drawstring sack. All was ready. She would complete this task then turn her attention to another problem that had to be resolved, but first things first. She closed her eyes and thought about the last time this concoction had been used.

It was late at night. The rain had pounded the earth with a fury. Oya, the Orisha of wind and rain, was enraged and had unleashed her ferocious tempest. She and her grandma huddled under a shabby umbrella and quickly crossed the soaked, muddy yard to enter the barn. They were solemn as they looked at the semiconscious Bethelee. Intent on what they had to do, they moved forward to the prone girl lying on the dirty hay. It wouldn't be easy but it had to be done. She could still hear the screams that echoed against the howling storm in that cold, damp barn. Terrible shrieks of anguish that no one would hear reverberated in the deserted, dark woods in Mississippi. The screeches had been endless. The pleading and begging for them to stop had turned into retched sobs of misery. But they had not stopped. They kept plowing onward until they had completed their task and then callously left the barn without looking back. What had happened on that desolate night had been for the best. She and her grandma had agreed that it was for the best.

Millie opened her eyes and turned to look out the window as she tightly clutched the velvet sack. She thought of her grandma.

"This is for the best, grandma. It's for the best," Millie swore.

CHAPTER 12

Josie opened the door. A small, wiry man with a receding hairline stood before her. He wore a brown overcoat and held a black briefcase.

"Mrs. Robert Brooks?" he enquired.

"Yes," Josie said hesitantly. She had no idea who this man was or why he was at her door.

"May I come in? I have a matter of utmost importance to discuss with you," as he took her acquiesce for granted and entered the house.

Josie was shocked at his brashness. Lisa had choice words for him.

"Who do you think you are barging in here without permission?" Lisa was outraged.

"May I sit?" he asked. "I'm sure my deplorable manners will be forgiven once I explain why I am here."

He waited expectantly for Josie to grant him permission to sit. Josie realized why he was waiting and gestured for him to do so.

"Have a seat," Josie said dully.

He sat on the sofa and set his briefcase on cushion next to him. Josie and Lisa sat in the armchairs facing him.

"My name is Arnold Wainscot. I am an attorney for Hartwell and Klein finance firm. Your late husband, Robert Brook, retained our firm to oversee his investment. Please accept my condolences for his recent passing," he said sincerely.

Josie and Lisa looked at each other in shock. Josie's head was spinning. What was he talking about? What investment? Rob had said nothing about an investment to her. Josie cleared her throat.

"I'm sorry but I don't know anything about an investment," Josie murmured.

"It's quite all right. It often happens that the grieving widow has no clue of what her late husband had done. It makes my job either joyous or miserable depending on the information I have to divulge. In this case, I am quite cheerful indeed," he said happily with a wide grin.

"Cheerful?" Lisa repeated. "What are you here to say?"

"That you, Mrs. Brooks, are the recipient of eight hundred thousand dollars as a result of your husband investing in the bottled water industry. He got in on the ground floor and is making a killing. Oh, I'm so sorry for my poor choice of words," he smiled benevolently.

Josie was speechless. She couldn't believe her ears.

"Eight hundred thousand dollars?" Josie said incredibly. "I can't believe it."

"Believe it. And your return is growing larger by the minute," Arnold said.

Lisa jumped out of her seat and hugged Josie.

"Your problems are solved, Josie. I'm so happy for you," Lisa said joyfully.

"Are you sure, Mr. Wainscot?" Josie asked breathlessly.

"I'm positive. Your husband took a gamble and it's paying off handsomely. You will never have to worry about money ever again, Mrs. Brooks," Arnold said pleasantly. "We at Hartwell and Klein will continue to watch over this investment judiciously, that is, if you wish to remain with us. We will advise you on the management of your investment and recommend options that are best suited for you. You will receive a substantial dividend check every month. I just have this document for you to review and sign and then we can release the funds to you. Please feel free to have your attorney read it before you sign it. We at Hartwell and Klein want all parties to feel completely comfortable about any transaction we conduct before you sign on the proverbial dotted line."

He pulled an official looking document from his briefcase and laid it on the cocktail table. He then closed his briefcase and stood up.

"I'm sure that this document will meet with your satisfaction. If not, please contact me immediately." He had laid his business card on the table as well. He walked briskly to the door. He paused and turned toward them. "Good day, ladies" he said congenially.

Josie rushed to the door to see him out.

"Goodbye, Mr. Wainscot, and thank you. Thank you so very much," Josie gushed.

He nodded his head and walked quickly to his car. Josie closed the door and looked at Lisa. They both screamed and jumped for joy.

Derek stood on the Brooklyn Bridge watching the rushing waves of the East River. He rested his gloved hands on the railing and wished that the churning water could give him the answers that he sought. There were so many questions that needed answers yet the main question—who killed his brother-in-laws—had been answered. He knew without a doubt who the culprit was. And the motive was obvious if you knew the people involved intimately. Even an intuitive, sharp-minded person would need to know these people personally to understand the reason behind the murders. He knew everyone involved very, very well. That's why what he had to do was so damn difficult. Why did he have to be the one to bring down the hatchet? Why didn't the previous detectives figure this case out and dispensed justice? He could only think that God meant for it to be this way. God wanted him to handle this situation. So be it. He was a civil servant of the court, honor bound to uphold society's laws and protect the people of this city. His decision of what he should do was made when he took his oath as an officer of this community. Regardless of who he may hurt, he knew what he had to do. Derek shoved his hands deep into his pockets and turned to walk back across the bridge and into what could only be a horrid mess.

"Josie, this solves your problem," Lisa said excitedly. "You can pay off Duncan and be free of him."

Lisa was sitting on the sofa, her legs crossed beneath her. Josie sat in the armchair across from Lisa and laughed at her obvious elation.

"Yes, I can," Josie responded, although the thought of being rid of Duncan did not give her the satisfaction that she had expected.

"I can't wait for him to get here and hear that you can pay him. The news will surely send him into a tailspin," Lisa said gleefully.

"I imagine it will. The news nearly took me out," Josie said.

"So Rob truly never mentioned any of this to you?" Lisa asked in awe.

"No. I guess he didn't want to get my hopes up if the investment was a bust," Josie said.

"But it wasn't. Your earnings from this venture will take care of you and the kids for the rest of your lives. I wouldn't have believed it had I not been here to hear it for myself. It's a miracle," Lisa said exuberantly.

"Yes, it is. I am so happy." Josie grinned. "The bottled water venture was the reason Rob borrowed money from Duncan. He knew his credit would not allow him to secure the money from the banks, so he turned to Duncan."

"He really was trying to take care of you and the kids, Josie," Lisa said. "He loved you very much."

"He did. He didn't always choose the best way to show it, but he loved us tremendously. And I miss him so much," Josie said sadly. "When I think of what he's done for us—" Josie began to cry softly. Lisa quickly moved to her side. Kneeling beside her chair, Lisa cupped Josie's hands in her.

"It's all right, Josie. You can cry all you want. Just know that I am here for you. And I'm not going anywhere," Lisa said softly.

Josie pulled a tissue out of her pocket and dried her eyes.

"It was just a moment of weakness. I'm okay now," Josie said between sniffles.

"Moments of sadness are to be expected. You've been through a horrible nightmare. It's going to take time for you to move on," Lisa empathized.

"I'm all right now. Rob came through like I always knew he would. And I am so grateful to him," Josie said. She stood up. "I have several errands to run before Duncan gets here. I'd better get going."

Lisa stood up too.

"You know, I think I'll take a nap. I didn't sleep well last night, but now I think I can sleep like a log," Lisa said through a yawn.

Josie chuckled as she went into the hall to get her coat off the rack.

"Where's my coat? I thought I hung it up on the coat rack," Josie was bemused.

Lisa was a bit uncomfortable.

"Sam came to pick it up, Josie. I'm not sure why they needed it, but I think they are on to something," Lisa explained.

"Really? Why would they want my coat?" Josie asked in bewilderment.

Lisa shrugged.

"I'm not sure. Sam would not elaborate," Lisa said. She hoped Josie's happiness over what had just occurred would prevent her from thinking the obvious.

"Alright. I'll wear this jacket instead," Josie said. She picked up her purse from the nearby table and hung it on her shoulder.

"I won't be gone long," Josie said as she opened the door.

""Okay," Lisa replied in relief. She had expected Josie to go ballistic. "You're alright with the police taking it?"

"Sure. I'm sure everything will work itself out. I just have a gut feeling," Josie said blithely.

"Well, I will trust your gut any day. I think I'll sleep here on the sofa until you get back," Lisa said.

"All right. Bye," Josie said.

"Bye," Lisa responded as she stretched out on the sofa. It didn't take her long to fall asleep. Her lips curved into a soft smile suggesting she was having a good dream.

There was an insistent pounding on Millie's front door. She slowly walked to the front to the house and peeped through the curtains of the large bay window. She saw who was at the door and turned to walk back to the kitchen.

"I know you're in there, Millie. Open this door." The pounding on the door was so hard that the frame shook.

Millie angrily retraced her steps to the door and yanked it open.

"What are you doing here? You're not welcome at my home," Millie shouted at the visitor.

Bethelee pushed her way into the house.

"I'm here to tell you to leave her alone," Bethelee said starkly.

"Leave who alone?" Millie demanded.

"You know damn well who I'm talking about. I won't allow you to ruin their life. History will not repeat itself," Bethelee asserted.

"You come to my house after all these years to issue a threat?" Millie was incredulous. "I haven't seen you in decades and when I do, you try to threaten me. Get out!"

"Not until I have your word, on grandma's grave, that you will not do anything cruel and heinous," Bethelee snapped.

"You will not come into my house talking trash. Leave!" Millie ordered.

"No. Not until I have your word. I want your oath, Millie; on grandma's grave," Bethelee countered.

"Or what?" Millie barked.

"Or you'll have me to deal with," Bethelee promised.

Millie burst out laughing. "Oh, well I'm truly scared," Millie said sarcastically.

"I mean it, Millie. I won't allow you—" Bethelee began.

Millie cut her off ruthlessly. "You couldn't help yourself. How do you expect to help someone else?" Millie said caustically. "We did what needed to be done. You were a spoiled, selfish tramp then and you haven't changed now. You left me and grandma to fend for ourselves and you didn't look back. We were poorer than church mice but you didn't care. You left and didn't leave so much as a nickel for us to buy a loaf of bread."

"You know why I left. You ruined me!" Bethelee screamed in anguish.

"We saved you," Millie said triumphantly.

"I was your sister, Millie. How could you do something so despicable to your sister? You should have tried to stick up for me," Bethelee cried.

"You were going down the wrong path. We had to do something to set you straight," Millie declared. "Grandma said it was for the best. And it was."

"For who? The best for grandma's twisted need to control everyone around her. And if she couldn't rule you, she would 'fix' you?" Bethelee said in anguish. "Is that sane?"

"It needed to be done," Millie said stubbornly. "You were out of control. You wouldn't listen to reason."

"I wanted to pursue a career as a singer. What was so wrong about that?" Bethelee argued.

"It was sinful. You were living the life of a slut," Millie accused.

"I was living the life that I wanted and not the life grandma wanted for me. She despised me for defying her and she made me pay the ultimate price for it," Bethelee said in contempt. "How I hated her for it. And I hated you too because you were just like her. And you still are."

"So it was. And so it shall be," Millie suddenly shouted.

"You're insane. You need help," Bethelee cried out. She looked at Millie in disbelief.

"The only thing I need is for you to leave my house and never, ever come back," Millie snarled.

Millie pushed Bethelee to the still opened door. Bethelee tried to fight against Millie's strength but her efforts were in vain. Millie gave her a final shove and

Bethelee stumbled onto the porch. Millie slammed the door shut.

Sam was extremely worried about Derek. After reading the reports on Derek's desk, he had a good idea of where Derek was headed. He opened his desk drawer and pulled out his own revolver and slid it into his holster. He wasn't sure what would happen but he wanted to be prepared. He then put on his coat and briskly walked to the elevators.

The quiet creak of the back door opening and closing did not awaken her. The drawstring of the burlap bag hung snugly to the sturdy wrist of its owner. Sure footsteps silently fell on the multicolored hall runner. Feet clad in old leather, low-heeled oxfords stopped briefly in the arched entryway of the living room. Moving forward quickly, they inadvertently kicked the leg of the table which awakened Lisa. Just as Lisa opened her mouth to scream, a gloved fist slammed across her face. Lisa was knocked out like a defeated boxer. Hands then stripped Lisa's jeans and underpants from her body and spread her legs wide. Gloved hands open a black, drawstringed bag and retrieved a small bottle and syringe. They inserted the syringe into the bottle, filled it then squirted liquid into the air to test the needle. Satisfied, the needle moved toward Lisa's vagina.

"No! Stop! You will not do this again. Never again."

CHAPTER 13

Derek used his key to enter Millie's house. He called out her name but there was no response. He knew that he should probably call Sam but decided to call him a little later. He wandered outside and looked around. He looked to his left and saw the infamous hoe protruding from the dirt in the vegetable garden. He smiled as he thought about telling Angie that the tool was still in one piece. He walked back into the house and sat down on the couch. He clasped his hands behind his head and leaned back. He thought about the case. Never in a million years would he have thought that it would come to this. But when he read the forensic reports and spoke to Sandra, the pieces just fell together. It was still a theory and his precious little evidence was circumstantial at best. But his gut told him that he was right. He just needed to get a confession. Easier said than done, he knew. But closure was needed for these hellish crimes. And he wouldn't rest until justice was served, no matter the cost. Sandra and Josie deserved no less. He was thinking of the tumultuous scene to come when the front door opened. Derek was instantly alert and grasped the handle of his revolver. Sam entered the house.

"Sam," Derek exclaimed. "What are you doing here?"

"I read the files and wasn't comfortable with you coming here by yourself," Sam said a little sheepishly.

"Sam, I told you I would be all right. I will be talking to a woman after all," Derek said.

"You will be talking to Millie. A whole other story entirely," Sam defended himself.

Derek chuckled. "Be that as it may, I still will be fine."

"I'm not leaving, Derek," Sam said flatly.

"Okay," Derek sighed. "Although I think your presence will make things more difficult."

"So be it. I'm staying," Sam retorted obstinately as he sat down in the adjacent armchair.

"I said stop," Bethelee screamed.

"Lisa," Angie exclaimed as she ran to the sofa.

"No. I must save her," Millie cried.

Millie pushed Angie back and tried to insert the needle into Lisa. Bethelee and Sandra both accosted Millie, straining to pull her away from Lisa. Bethelee and Sandra tousled with Millie as Angie crawled back to Lisa and heaved her off the sofa, dragging her across the floor. She collapsed over Lisa protectively and watched as Sandra and Bethelee struggled with Millie. Millie was strong. Her anger fueled her might giving her the strength of ten. Sandra and Bethelee held tightly to Millie's arms but Millie flayed them away as though they were flies. Bethelee fell against the coffee table and Sandra tumbled backward onto the floor. Millie turned and looked at Angie as she held Lisa in her arms. Millie took a step toward Lisa. Bethelee rose up and knocked the syringe out of Millie's hand. Millie screamed in anger.

"You won't stop me," Millie shouted.

"Yes, I will. I won't let you ruin her life like you ruined mine," Bethelee screamed. "You and grandma destroyed any chance I had of having a family of my own. I won't let you do that to Lisa. It's over, Millie."

"Grandma would want me to do what's right. It's for the best. Lisa will understand. You understood, Bethelee. It was for the best," Millie said irrationally.

"I never understood. I never understood how you could be a part of making me barren. Relegating me to a life of being childless so you and grandma could avoid embarrassment should I become pregnant and wasn't married," Bethelee exclaimed. "How could you be so cruel and cold? You butchered me then left me alone in that cold, dark barn to cry myself into exhaustion. I hated you then and I hate you now. And I won't allow you to bestow upon Lisa the same wretched misery that has tormented me."

"You can't stop me," Millie yelled as she bent to pick up the discarded syringe. She moved toward Lisa who was still unconscious. Angie moved in front of Lisa to protect her.

"But I can."

Duncan was across the room in what seemed like a flash of black lightning, his black cape billowing behind him. He wrestled the needle from Millie's grasp then flung her across the room.

"No! No!" Millie screamed at Duncan as she landed in a heap on the floor. Her eyes danced in wild frenzy. "How dare you?"

"How dare you? She's your daughter, for Christ's sake," Duncan shouted.

"You'll pay. Mark my words. You all will pay," Millie shouted as she scrambled to her feet. Millie knew she was no match for Duncan. She fled through the door just as her eldest daughter was coming through it, pushing Josie against the door jamb. Josie was holding a brown grocery bag and its contents spilled onto the floor. Josie looked at everyone in confusion.

"What's going on?" Josie asked in shock.

Duncan crossed the room to embrace Josie.

"Are you all right, darling?" he asked.

Josie nodded affirmatively.

Duncan's comment caused Josie's sisters to look at each other in surprise and bafflement. Angie had draped an area rug over Lisa's waist and thighs for privacy. Sandra moved to kneel beside them and hugged Lisa.

"Aunt Bethelee?" Josie said.

Bethelee shakily rose from the floor.

"Yes, Josie. It's me and we have a lot to tell you. But first, perhaps you would kindly introduce us to your brave knight," Bethelee smiled kindly.

All eyes turned to Josie expectantly.

"Goodbye," Josie called out to Angie as she hurried down the walkway to the car.

Sandra touched Josie's shoulder as she too prepared to leave.

"I wish I could stay longer but I should get home to Jimmy and the kids," Sandra said gently.

"Of course you should. Lisa and I will be fine. Mama will not come back. I think her self-perseverance has kicked in and she won't risk returning," Josie said.

"Hmm, in the end, Mama will always look out for herself," Sandra surmised.

"But it doesn't hurt to have a gallant knight here to protect you," Bethelee smiled as she joined them at the door. Bethelee and Josie hugged for a moment.

"No, it doesn't," Josie grinned. "I'm finding that I rather like his surprise visits."

"Thank goodness he arrived. I'd hate to think what would have happened had he not shown up," Sandra said. They all looked at Duncan lounging on the sofa flipping through a magazine.

"I think you may want to consider his suit. Good ones are hard to come by. And I think he's a keeper," Bethelee said.

Josie only smiled at her comment.

"I will come to see you at Angie's. You will be here for a while, won't you?" Josie asked.

"Yes. I will be here," Bethelee answered. She knew there was still work to be done.

"Good." Josie said.

Bethelee and Sandra passed through the door and joined Angie at the car. They all got into the car, waved then drove off. Josie slowly closed the door and turned to look at Duncan. If only they knew that Duncan was not pursuing her. He only wanted his money. He saw her family leave and immediately rose to cross the room to her side.

"It's been a very stressful day. Come. Sit with me and relax. It's a wee bit chilly in here. I will make up a fire," Duncan said as he urged her to sit on the sofa. He spread a fluffy cotton throw across her lap, tucked it around her then turned to lay the fire.

Josie liked the way he fussed over her. It made her feel safe and secure. She watched him squat before the fireplace and arranged the wood and kindle. He had removed his cape and she could see his firm muscles through his black silk shirt. They moved fluidly as he expertly laid the fire. His masculine physique spoke volumes of his ability to protect what he held close and dear. His large hands so casually placed the logs on the grate. Those same hands could just as easily crush someone's neck. Even as she shivered at the deadly thought, she was inexplicably drawn to that same powerful, earthy sexuality. Somewhere deep inside of her, she knew she shouldn't be attracted to him but she was. She couldn't seem to help it. She wanted to feel those hands on her body holding and caressing her. She looked at his strong profile, the straight nose and full lips. She had seen those lips pulled into an uncompromising rigid line. He would brook no resistance to what he wanted. But she had also seen those same lips relaxed into a lazy, lopsided smile that could charm her into laughing with him. She wanted to taste his sensual lips. She wanted to know his kiss. She never thought that she would experience sexual urges again now that Rob was gone. But here they were and she wasn't sure how to handle them. He lit a match and tossed it onto the kindle. It immediately caught and a roaring flame began consuming the wood. He turned and gave her a roguish smile.

"It works every time," he said impishly. He rose and sat next to her, placing his arm around her shoulders. She allowed the intimate gesture because quite frankly, she was too drained to oppose him. And she liked being snuggled in his cocoon.

"I love sitting by a fire. It makes me feel safe," she said.

"You are safe. I will never let anything horrible happen to you and Lisa," Duncan murmured.

She looked up at him. He could see the perplexity in her hazel eyes.

"But why, Duncan? We're nothing to you except the means to the end of a successful business transaction," she asked.

"Little do you know you are so much more than that," he answered softly.

His answer left her even more confused and she wasn't sure how to respond. But there was one thing that she wanted to say to him once again.

"Thank you for saving Lisa. I am so grateful to you. I don't want to even consider what would have happened had you not arrived when you did," she said.

"You don't have to thank me, I—" he began.

"Yes, I do. You came to our rescue without even knowing we needed you. I will never be able to thank you enough," she said. "What can I do to repay you?"

"Nothing. I would do it a thousand times again and I would want nothing from you, except perhaps your friendship. Will you be my friend, Josie?" His forefinger tilted her chin to meet his gaze. "I don't have many people in my life that I can truly call friend. Will you be my friend?"

How could she deny his request? During a time of terror and turmoil, he had been the epitome of composure and rationality. Upon dispatching Millie posthaste, he picked up a still unconscious Lisa and bounded up the stairs effortlessly, placing her on the bed in the room Josie indicated. He then retreated to the living room, giving Josie and her sisters' time to settle Lisa. When they returned to the living room, Duncan and Bethelee were having a pleasant conversation. Josie knew that she would have to speak to Bethelee's comment regarding Duncan but she was uncertain of what to say. However, Duncan had smoothly addressed the situation by saying he was an associate of Robert's and had only recently heard of his passing. He came by because he had wanted to convey his condolences in person. It wasn't an out and out lie. He was Rob's associate. Josie was just glad that her family had accepted his explanation and thanked him profusely for saving Lisa. He had done so much for her. In all good conscious, she couldn't refuse his request and she really didn't want to. She wanted to get to know him better.

"Yes, I would be honored to be your friend," she said softly.

He grinned happily and she was glad that her answer had made him so happy. She could make him even happier by sharing her good news with him.

"I can repay your money. I have the means to do so now," Josie said. She looked into his suddenly shuttered eyes. She couldn't tell if he were glad to hear the news or not. He didn't react as though he was pleased.

Damn! How the hell did she come up with the funds. He was counting on her not having them to elongate his pursuit of her. How was he going to continue to see her if she paid off the debt?

"Duncan? Did you hear me? I can repay Rob's loan from you." Josie reiterated.

He removed his arm from her shoulders and leaned forward, resting his elbows on his knees. His fingers rubbed his forehead. Josie immediately missed the warm haven his arm had created.

"Yes, I heard you," he mumbled. "But you didn't have to incur a debt in order to repay me. I had no problem in waiting."

"That isn't how you made it appear to me. I got the impression that patience was not your strong suit," Josie said as she frowned.

"I would have," he muttered.

"Well, now you don't have to," she said.

He removed his hand from his temples and looked at her.

"How did you come up with the money, if you don't mind my asking," Duncan inquired.

Josie shrugged as she crossed her arms.

"It's really ironic but I am the recipient of Rob's investment," she said.

"I don't understand," he said confusedly.

"Rob borrowed the money from you to buy into an emerging bottled water company. His investment turned out to be money well spent. His shares have turned a phenomenal profit. I am now a very rich lady," Josie grinned.

Duncan looked at her smiling face and could not hold back a grin of his own. He was actually very happy for her. She and her children were financially secure. He leaned back and rested his arm on the back of the sofa.

"I'm very happy for you, Josie. You can raise your family without financial worries. It is a huge anxiety removed from your dainty shoulders," he said.

There goes that achingly alluring smile of his coupled with his sexy accent. How was she to keep a straight head when he appeared so tempting, inviting her to indulge in things that she shouldn't. Josie averted her glance and shifted uncomfortably.

"Er...yes. It solves a lot of problems. The money should be transferred into my account in a day or two. I can have a check for you then, or do you prefer cash?" she queried.

He leaned closer to her.

"Cash would be preferable," he whispered into her ear.

Josie jumped up. She wanted to put some space between them. She was nervous and felt that she shouldn't get too close to him.

"All righty then. I'll take care of it," she said uneasily.

"Come sit down, Josie."

"I think I'll check on Lisa," she hedged.

"Lisa is fine. Come here," he ordered.

The firmness of his tone made her want to bolt but she plucked up the courage to return to the sofa. She nervously sat at the opposite end of it. He reached across the sofa, grasped her arm and pulled her close to his side. Encircling her shoulders, he gently laid her head on his chest.

"There. Isn't this better? Much more comfy," he said softly.

Josie sat stiffly as she tried to resist the temptation to relax in his arms. But her resolve could not stand up to his tender caress on her shoulder or the deep, mellow tenor of his voice. The atmosphere that he had created was so restful and she desperately craved peace. She closed her eyes, sighed deeply, and gave into the cozy tranquility. Duncan felt and heard her resignation. He smiled and lightly kissed the top of her head. He held her even tighter. Laying his head back against the sofa, he closed his eyes. This was how it was supposed to be. Josie nestled in his arms without worry or fear. He would tend to her, protect her from all harm because he cared too much about her not to. An odd way to think of it but that was the gist of it. She had become very important to him in a very short period of time and he didn't want to lose her. He wouldn't lose her. He wanted to be in her life, and after what had happened today, she could not very well make him stay away. He realized, even if she didn't, that she needed him and he wasn't about to go anywhere. He didn't care that she could repay the money. He wouldn't take it. He didn't want it. He just wanted her. He didn't know where these feelings were leading. He would just have to wait to find out. In the meantime, he would enjoy being with his Josie.

∾

Jimmy sat on the couch in horror as he listened to Sandra and Angie's account of what had transpired.

"Did you call the police?" Jimmy asked.

"I called the station but Derek wasn't there," Angie said. "I didn't want to tell other policeman about it before talking to Derek."

"I'm just glad you agreed to stay here with us. I don't want to you to be at home by yourself," Sandra said.

"I paged Derek and so did the station. I should hear from him soon," Angie said hopefully.

"Thank God for this Duncan character. But who is he?" Jimmy asked.

"He's a friend of Josie's," Angie answered.

"No. He said he was an associate of Rob's," Sandra said.

"Whatever! I'm just glad he showed up when he did. I'm not sure if we could have held Mama off," Angie exclaimed.

"Aunt Bethelee and I were not faring well. Mama was so strong," Sandra said as she shuddered at the memory.

"And a little crazy as well," Angie said dully. "She refused to listen. She really thought that she was doing the right thing."

"I think she lost it, babe," Jimmy said as held Sandra close.

"Angie!" Derek called out as he ran into the house.

Angie stood up and ran into Derek's arms.

"I'm all right," she sighed.

"Are you sure?" Derek questioned as he held her tightly.

"Yes, I'm sure. Lisa is the one who bore the brunt of Mama's craziness," Angie said as she pulled out of Derek's arms. She led him to the sofa and they both sat down.

"I got your page. What happened?" Derek asked brusquely.

Sandra and Angie related what had happened. Even Jimmy interjected a few cynical comments.

"This is unbelievable. And who is Duncan?" Derek asked mystified.

"A friend of Rob's. He came to pay his respects. Josie was rather sketchy about him," Sandra frowned. "In fact, Josie didn't introduce him at all. He did all of the talking."

"Well, thank goodness he showed up when he did," Angie said.

"I still don't know what could have set her off like this?" Derek asked upon hearing the sordid details.

"Who knows?" Sandra answered quietly. "But obviously she intended to do the same to Lisa as she and her grandmother had done to Aunt Bethelee."

"How is Brat?" Derek asked anxiously.

"She was still unconscious when we left Josie's. She moaned briefly but did not wake up. Duncan carried her upstairs and we put her to bed," Angie answered.

"But why?" Derek asked again. "There has to be a reason. Something made her think that such horrific measures were called for."

"At this point, does it really matter?" Jimmy said forcefully. "She's whacked and she must be stopped."

"I would like to know what set her off. It could help in diffusing the anger she's feeling. Her efforts were thwarted so you know she's furious," Derek surmised.

"I can't imagine Lisa doing anything that would enrage Mama to the point of harming her," Sandra said.

"She's not thinking rationally. She's operating purely on emotions. Emotions that are driving her to ruin her daughter's life, if we don't stop her," Derek said.

"He's right," Angie said. "Mama thinks she's doing the right thing. Her love for Lisa, and I guess all of us, has become twisted and cruel. I wish I knew why."

"Our grandmother," Bethelee said as she entered the living room.

"Aunt Bethelee!" Sandra and Angie spoke in unison.

Bethelee stood in the archway just inside of the room. She stood resolutely with her hands clasped at her stomach.

"Millie is the replica of our grandma Molly. From a small child, Millie idolized our grandmamma," Bethelee calmly stated. "Grandma could do no wrong in Millie's eyes. Millie worshipped the air grandma Molly breathed, and she sought grandma's affection and approval by acting like a miniature Molly. Grandma would reward Millie's behavior with unlimited love to strengthen her hold on her. This is the result of her influence on Millie."

Everyone sat in stunned silence as they processed what Bethelee said. Finally, Angie stood and crossed to Bethelee, taking her coat, purse, and suitcase.

"Let me take these for you. How did you get here?" Angie said as she seated her in a comfortable chair. "Derek and I were going to pick you up."

"A taxi takes you wherever you want to go," Bethelee smiled. "I wanted to save you the trip. I felt you would still be at Sandra's home. I know you had a lot to discuss."

"That's for sure," Jimmy grimaced.

"What should we do, Aunt Bethelee?" Sandra asked. "She's our mother but we have a responsibility to protect Lisa. She has to be stopped."

"I don't know," Bethelee said as she shook her head sadly. "Millie is full of self-righteous anger. She's livid that her plot to violate Lisa was foiled. But she will not stop trying until she is forced to concede," Bethelee said scornfully.

"I was over at Mama's place when I got your page," Derek said slowly.

"Why?" Angie asked.

"Because I wanted to see if my theory was correct," Derek answered.

"What theory?" Jimmy questioned.

"I can't get into it but I think I should go back there," Derek stated.

"No!" Angie exclaimed. "You can't."

"It's too dangerous for you to go there by yourself, Derek. You don't know what you would be walking into," Jimmy said forcefully.

"I have to go. Besides, Sam was with me. I'll go tomorrow, giving Mama some time to cool off," Derek reasoned.

"Mama is not going to cool off overnight. That won't happen anytime soon," Sandra retorted.

"It's too dangerous, Derek. Please don't go," Angie pleaded.

"I have to, babe," Derek said softly as he pulled Angie against his side. Her body was stiff with trepidation. "Mama likes me. She won't try to hurt me."

"Man, it's that kind of thinking that will get you killed. I'm going with you and I'm calling Sam," Jimmy said flatly.

Derek shook his head negatively.

"No. Seeing you with me or the police would only make her suspicious and guarded," Derek said.

"After what happened today, seeing any of us would put her back up. You can't go alone," Jimmy argued.

"I can't sit on what I need to do, Jimmy. I have to talk to her," Derek reiterated.

"Give it a few days, Derek. Maybe we will see a positive change in Mama. Perhaps she will be more approachable by then," Sandra suggested.

Derek hesitated. Their arguments made reasonable sense but they were not dealing with a sensible, rational woman, not at this point. He wanted to strike while the iron was hot. To confront her when her pious passions were raging. Maybe he would get a confession through her impulsive rant. He didn't want her to calm down and methodically plan her next attack. He couldn't allow her any advantages. His gut was telling him to talk to Millie now. He looked into Angie's face and saw fear and dread. He hated deceiving her. He looked away from her.

"All right. I'll wait," Derek said.

Derek felt Angie sag against him as anxiety left her body.

"Thank God," Angie breathed.

"It's the right decision, man," Jimmy said. "Let Mama settle down a bit."

Derek smiled grimly and looked at Bethelee. Her stare pierced him sharply, seemingly seeing right through him. He could see in her eyes that she didn't believe him. She knew his thoughts because she knows Millie. Although her perception was unsettling, it didn't change his mind. He knew what he had to do.

CHAPTER 14

Derek and Angie ushered Bethelee into their home and were perfectly hospitable to her. They had seen to her every need. Neither of them had brought up the topic of Millie again. They appeared exhausted of the subject. Bethelee understood that. Millie could be extremely tiring and depleting. Dealing with her could drain your energy and nothing would come from your efforts. Derek and Angie had long since gone to bed and the house was eerily silent. But Bethelee was restless and sleep eluded her. She stood before the bedroom window and stared at the dark night. It was beginning to rain. The wet, slick streets were abandoned. Everyone had scurried indoors to avoid the inclement weather. Bethelee pulled her robe more tightly about her as she viewed the damp landscape before her. She could hear the raindrops falling from the gutters onto soaked cement. It reminded her of another storm, at another time when she was a young teenager and her bright future had been stripped from her. It had been many years since she had allowed her mind to remember that horrible night when a raven could be heard crowing against the howling wind of the storm's wrath. She had refused to recall the circumstances that had changed her life irrevocably. All due to what she now understood to be the sanity of a deranged woman. She had lain there listening to the raindrops falling from the roof of the old barn to the sodden ground. Battered. Broken. Defeated. No matter how hard she tried, she could not erase the events of that fateful night from her memory. It always came back to haunt her, to taunt her. She had hoped that time had assuaged Millie's temperament. Hoped that it had softened her heart and smoothed out the hardened edges of Millie's inflexible rationale. But time had not been a friend in this regard. Millie was the same woman she had been forty-eight years ago. She and grandmamma had ruined an eighteen-year-old's life in the single swoop of their hands. How she had raged against the injustice of it all. How she had hated them. It had taken many years for her to forgive them. But the bitterness and loneliness of not having a family still remained. Those feelings would probably follow her to her grave. But now was an opportunity to prevent history from repeating itself. This time, the story would have a different ending, a lifesaving ending. This time Millie would not triumph. This time she would win.

Millie crept into her house from the back door. She had needed to wait until the middle of the night before she could trust it was safe to return home. She was wet and hungry. But most of all she was incensed, livid that she was prevented from doing what needed to be done. How dare they presume to judge her actions to be wrong and unjust? They knew nothing of preventing sin from raising its ugly heads. She was the one that had to safeguard the future from the results of reckless behavior of the present.

She moved into the kitchen and placed the pouch that she clutched in her hand onto the table. Her hands trembled as she opened it and peered inside.

"You'll be put to good use yet. Don't you worry," she mumbled. "I'll see to it."

Josie turned her head on the pillow and continued to sleep. Duncan sat in her bedroom recliner and watched her protectively. She was such a lovely woman. Any man would be crazy not to recognize it and want her for himself. And he wanted her. There wasn't anything that he wouldn't do for her. It had been a stroke of luck that he had arrived at precisely the time that her family needed him. He had quickly assessed what was happening and acted instinctively, thinking only to diffuse the volatile situation before harm could be done to Lisa. Josie's mother was a piece of work. What mother would want to hurt her own daughter? What could have driven her to such demonic behavior? He didn't have the answers but he did know that he would be damned if he'd let any harm come to Josie or her family. They were her heart, which meant they were dear to him. It's a little funny but he now realized just how much he cared about Josie. And he would do anything to make her happy. And if that meant protecting her family, then that's what he would gladly do.

Dawn was breaking over the horizon. The rain had stopped and he could see tiny rays of the sun peeking above the distant mountains. It had been a long night, made even longer by his futile efforts to force his large frame to fit into her small recliner. He guessed the chair was of a normal size. He was just a very big man. He grunted as he twisted his massive body, trying to find a comfortable position. It would take a contortionist to sit in this chair.

His groans must have awakened Josie for she was lying in bed smiling at him. He saw her lips curving upward and he sighed dramatically.

"How is a man to get a decent night's sleep in this torturous contraption?" he bemoaned.

"It's a chair. And it was built for a smaller person," she smiled.

"Obviously," he grumbled.

He pulled himself from the stranglehold of the chair and moved to sit beside her on the bed.

"I think you're right. I'll just have to sleep in a bed tonight," he said lightly. His crimson eyes twinkled merrily.

"But I don't have another available bedroom in the house," Josie said uncertainly.

"This bed," he indicated the bed he was sitting on, "will do just fine." He smiled wickedly.

"Oh no. That's not a good idea," she said hurriedly. She was not about to allow him entry into her bed. She knew her defenses would melt if he so much as kissed her cheek.

"No? Well, we'll figure something out because I'm not going anywhere. I intend to stay here until this ghastly matter with your mother is straightened out," he replied firmly.

Josie pushed herself into a sitting position. He slowly leaned toward her. Her eyes were wide as she held her breath, waiting for his kiss. But he reached around her and fluffed her pillows to support her back.

"There. Much more comfy, hmm?" he said silkily.

Josie slowly exhaled as she nodded affirmatively. She felt oddly deflated. She had anticipated his kiss. She'd wanted it to happen. She shouldn't have, but she did. Oh brother. What was wrong with her? She shouldn't be concerned about whether Duncan wanted to kiss her. She had more important things to think about.

"I need to get up and check on Lisa," she mumbled. She tried to throw the covers back to get up but he was sitting on them. She looked at him in askance. He got the message and stood up.

"I checked on her a little bit ago and she was asleep. However, I know you want to see for yourself," he said.

"Yes, I do. She went through so much yesterday. I want to make sure she's all right," she said as she stood and put on her robe.

"Of course. I would expect nothing less of you," he responded.

"Duncan," she began.

"Yes," he replied.

"I hope you know how grateful I am to you. I don't—"

"Enough. You have paid me with your thanks. I know how you feel," Duncan said gently.

"You do? I mean, how—"

"There's someone I am very close to. I know how I would feel if they were to become lost to me," he finished.

Josie waited for him to say more but he remained silent. There was so much that she didn't know about him. Who was he, really? How did he come to be in America? How did he live? Where did he live? And would the answers relieve her mind or give her more cause for concern? She wasn't sure but knew she wanted to find out. She wanted to know all about him—the good, awful, and in between. She needed to know what made him who he was. She cared. She realized that she really cared about him. He stood there watching her closely. His amber eyes were flashing sparks. She suddenly had trouble catching her breath.

"I'd better go to Lisa," she blurted out.

He nodded.

Josie walked toward the door but stopped when he moved to follow her. She looked at him cautiously.

"I think I should visit her alone. You don't mind, do you?" she said carefully. She didn't want to offend him.

"No, not at all. Visit your sister. I'll check the house and grounds to make sure all is secure," he said.

"The grounds?" Josie smiled. "You make it seem as though I live on a huge estate."

He shrugged. "I am Scottish. We speak a little differently than Americans."

"I like it." She smiled as she went out of the bedroom.

"And I like you," he said softly. He then picked up his cape from the back of his chair and threw it over his shoulders. He checked his waistband to ensure that his dagger was in place, and then left the room.

Derek slowly turned his key in the bolt lock of Millie's front door. Pushing the door open, he entered the house. It was gloomy inside. All of the window shades were drawn and the house was deathly silent.

"Mama!" Derek called.

Silence.

"Mama!" he called again as he made his way to the kitchen.

Still silence.

He pushed open the swinging door and stood in the middle of the kitchen. There was no one there. He moved to her bedroom which was on the first floor. Walking down the hall, the old wooden floor creaked with each gingerly step he took. Her bedroom door was closed. He knocked.

"Mama!" he called out.

There was no response. His hand curved around the door knob and pushed inward. The window drapes were pulled, casting an eerie darkness throughout the room. He looked at the made-up bed and doubted if Millie had slept in it last night. He noticed a pile of papers on it. He glanced at an old photograph and picked it up for closer inspection. It was a picture of a cabin. Millie and her daughters were standing in front of the porch. The girls were adolescents. Lisa looked to be about three or four. There were smiles on all of the faces, even Millie's. He didn't recognize the cabin but he had a vague memory of Angie mentioning it. He slid the photograph into his jacket pocket. Maybe Millie was hiding out there until things settled down.

It would be worth checking into. He gave a cursory look at the other papers but they were just old recipes. He turned to leave the room when something caught his eye. He looked backed toward the dresser and saw something protruding from the top drawer. Crossing to the dresser, he saw that it was a velvet string. He pulled the drawer open and saw it was a drawstring attached to a pouch. He opened the pouch and saw that it was empty. He remembered Angie telling him that Mama had pulled a wicked looking needle from a velvet pouch when she attacked Lisa yesterday. Mama was on the move. And Lisa was in danger. He threw the pouch down on the dresser and ran out.

Lisa moved across the living room and sighed deeply. She folded her arms and looked at the dark, murky clouds and knew they were in for a lot more rain and it would most likely begin to snow. Well, that was just as well because her mood matched the weather perfectly. Had it not been for Duncan her life would have been ruined. Never had she imagined that Mama would go to such lengths to control her, destroy her. What had she done that warranted such condemnation? Why had Mama thought that she was wayward? She wasn't wild, flirtatious, or promiscuous. She simply liked to sing. What was wrong in pursuing it? She was damn good at it. Why couldn't Mama see that? She thinks I'm like Aunt Bethelee. But Aunt Bethelee's life turned out to be pretty good. She became a very successful singer and traveled the world doing what she loves. What's wrong with that? It's not wrong doing what you love, what you were born to do. Why can't Mama see that? She sighed again and made a decision. She needed some air. Josie was taking a bath and Duncan had gone out to get reinforcements, whatever that meant. She had to get out of the house. She would go for a walk before the rain came. It would clear her head. She crossed to the coat rack, grabbed her jacket, and left the house.

Just moments later, Josie wandered down the steps and moved into the living room. She looked around. Not seeing Lisa, she shrugged her shoulders and walked into the kitchen. She still didn't see Lisa.

"Lisa," she called out. There was no response. Josie became nervous. She ran up the staircase and stumbled midway. She quickly righted herself and clambered the remaining steps. "Lisa!" she yelled as she skidded into Lisa's bedroom. There was no answer and no Lisa. "Oh my God," she exclaimed. Leaving the bedroom, she ran down the hall to make a call from the telephone on the hall table. She quickly dialed just as her front door opened.

"Josie," Sandra called out as she entered the house.

Josie slammed the telephone down and bolted to the top of the stairs.

"Sandra," Josie breathed heavily.

Sandra looked up at Josie in concern.

"What's wrong," Sandra asked anxiously.

Josie ran down the steps.

"I can't find Lisa."

"What do you mean you can't find her?" Sandra nearly shouted.

"I came downstairs after taking a bath and I couldn't find her," Josie said miserably.

"She has to be here somewhere," Sandra said insistently.

"I looked upstairs and down. She's not here," Josie said fearfully.

"Maybe she's out back. She loves your rose garden," Sandra suggested.

"I hadn't thought of that. Let's go look," Josie said hopefully.

They quickly walked to the back door and went outside. They looked all around the yard and side of the house.

"I can't believe she's not here," Sandra exclaimed. "She knows she shouldn't leave the house."

"Maybe she thought she would be safer outside of the house rather than in," Josie was searching for an explanation. "But why didn't she say something before taking off?"

"It's just like her not to. Lisa doesn't always think before doing," Sandra said.

They trooped back into the house.

"We have to call Derek," Sandra said. "He needs to start a search for her."

"What's going on?"

Duncan stood in the kitchen doorway. Josie had not heard him enter but she was glad he was there.

"Lisa is gone. We searched the house but she's nowhere to be found."

"I'm calling Derek now," Sandra said as she moved to the telephone hanging on the wall.

As Sandra spoke on the phone, Duncan pulled Josie aside. "Where would she have gone?" he asked. His accent was extremely pronounced in his worry.

"She likes walking in the park down the street or window shopping downtown. Both are within walking distance," Josie said worriedly. "She probably just wanted to get some air and space."

"Perhaps. But it is dangerous for her to be alone," he murmured.

Sandra hung up the phone.

"He's not in the office. I had him paged," Sandra said. "I'm sure he will call in soon, considering the circumstances."

"We have to go look for her. We're wasting time just standing here," Josie cried out.

"I will look for her," Duncan said. "She cannot have gone far on foot."

"I'm going with you. I can't sit here doing nothing," Sandra said.

"I'm going too," Josie said adamantly.

"I can go faster alone. Besides, I doubt if you will want to ride on the back of my bike," he stated.

"Your bike?" Josie questioned.

"My motorcycle," he clarified.

Just then, the doorbell rang. Josie hurried to the answer the door.

"Derek! Thank God. Lisa is missing," she exclaimed. She led him back to the kitchen.

They entered the kitchen and Derek's eyes immediately focused on Duncan. Derek looked at him hard, taking his measure. Duncan stood tall, broad, and majestic, returning his stare sardonically. He extended his hand.

"I am Duncan," he said. He waited for Derek to take his hand.

Derek hesitated for what seemed like an eternity. Finally Derek did so.

"Derek," Derek muttered. This was the man that had saved Lisa. He knew that he should be more gracious to him but damn it, it galled him that Duncan was the one who had come to Lisa's rescue and not himself. He was the one who was supposed to be Sir Galahad in this family. And the fact that it was Brat's life that Duncan had saved made Derek feel even more resentful of him. He was Lisa's big brother. He was the one that she looked to for help. He was the one who was supposed to change all her wrongs to rights. He did not like the idea of another man usurping his place.

"Get over it," Duncan challenged him.

Everyone looked between Derek and Duncan in baffled askance. Duncan knew what he was thinking which made Derek want to punch him in the face.

"Shall we check our egos at the door and proceed?" Duncan demanded.

Derek was shocked that Duncan dared to openly disparage him. It was unnerving and damn smug of him. But he was right. His focus should be on Lisa and not his uncharacteristic jealousy of Duncan.

"I went to Mama's house this morning and she wasn't there. I can only guess that she has been out waiting for an opportune moment to snatch Lisa," he began. "The longer Lisa is missing, the more probable it is that Millie has nabbed her. I received your message, Sandra, and I placed an APB on Millie and Lisa. Cops are scouring the city looking for them."

"We were about to go searching for her when you arrived," Sandra said. "We need to go now."

"Before you do, I want to show you something," Derek said. He pulled the old photograph from his pocket and laid it on the table. "Do you remember this place?"

Josie picked up the photograph and she and Sandra scrutinized it.

"It's our old cabin," Josie said. "We haven't been there in years."

"Didn't Mama sell it?" Sandra asked.

Josie shook her head. "She was going to but she changed her mind. She said it held too many memories for her to sell it," Josie replied.

"Memories of what? We were seldom there," Sandra wondered.

"I had thought that Mama might hold up there until things cooled down. But if she has Lisa, then the odds have just increased that she would go there. She's banking on you not thinking of it," Derek reasoned.

"And this cabin fits the bill," Josie said worriedly. "It's isolated in the woods. No neighbors for at least two miles."

"There's no time to spare. Josie, do you remember how to get there?" Duncan asked.

"Yes," she answered.

"So do I," Sandra piped up.

"Good," Derek said and looked at Duncan. "The girls will come with me. We can handle this from here on out." Derek's tone was stern.

"The forest is densely populated with trees. Eventually you will have to park your car and go on foot. I can make faster time on my bike," Duncan countered.

"I'm going with Duncan," Josie announced inflexibly. Her tone brooked no argument. She looked at Duncan. "You do have a second helmet?"

"But of course," Duncan looked at her as the side of his mouth tilted upward.

Derek didn't want Duncan coming with them but there was little he could do about it. It was obvious that Josie wanted Duncan with her. They all moved toward the front door, pausing just long enough for Josie to put on her coat. Derek opened the door and encountered Angie's raised fist ready to knock.

"Angie!" Derek said.

Angie looked apprehensively at everyone. Aunt Bethelee was standing beside her.

"What's going on?" Angie said fearfully.

"Come on. We'll tell you on the way," Sandra said. "Wait. Aunt Bethelee, stay here at the house in case Lisa comes back here."

"Alright. Please be careful. Millie is deranged and there's no telling what she will do," Bethelee cautioned.

"I'll radio for a patrol car to park out front as well," Derek said.

"We'll be back with Lisa soon," Angie said to Bethelee.

Bethelee nodded. They all ran to their cars. Duncan settled Josie on the back of his gleaming black and silver bike.

"It's beautiful," Josie complimented.

"My reinforcement. Hold tight," Duncan barked as he mounted the powerful motorcycle.

Josie tightened her arms around his waist and they roared off.

CHAPTER 15

"Come on," Millie yelled at Lisa as she tugged on Lisa's arm.

"Please, Mama. Let me go," Lisa pleaded.

Millie said nothing as she continued to pull Lisa through the woods. Lisa stumbled and fell. She cried out and grabbed her ankle. Millie looked down at her in disgust.

"Get up," Millie snarled.

Lisa held her ankle.

"I can't. I've hurt my ankle," Lisa wailed.

"I said get up," Millie snapped.

Millie yanked Lisa upward and pushed her forward. Lisa screamed in pain. Millie grasped Lisa's shoulders and squeezed them hard. She looked deep into Lisa's frightened eyes.

"This is for the best. You'll see. It's for the best," Millie said fervently.

Derek drove at breakneck speed. He had to get to Lisa before it was too late. Sam had caught up to them and was right behind him. He had spoken to Sam by radio and brought him up to date as he drove. From what he could see in his rearview mirror, Sam had picked up Jimmy from somewhere along the way. Duncan and Josie had sped past them a while ago and was a good distance ahead of him. However, his siren allowed him to keep them in view as traffic pulled aside for him. They soon were on the road that led to the privately owned forest land. It wouldn't be long before they would have to leave the car and resort to foot travel.

"Turn right at the next dirt road, Derek," Sandra instructed.

He did so. Suddenly, the forest seemed to close in on both sides of them. The road was bumpy and deserted. It twisted and bent like the wicked witch's crooked cane. Then it came to an abrupt dead end. Duncan and Josie went off-road and continued on, twisting and weaving around the centuries-old, tall, thick trees. Everyone exited the cars.

"Sam, Jimmy, let's go. You ladies stay here. It's too dangerous for you to go any further," Derek said.

"Oh, I don't think so," Sandra said. "You want me to come this far and then stay behind? It ain't happening."

"Sandra, please. This is no time for an argument," Derek said.

"Exactly," Angie interjected. "So we'd better start moving."

Angie and Sandra began trudging through the forest. Jimmy and Sam followed. Derek sighed deeply. He had no choice but to follow as well.

Millie continued to pull a struggling Lisa. She pushed, prodded, and dragged Lisa on the cold, leaf-covered ground. Lisa tried grabbing a stout tree branch to halt their progress. But Millie hammered Lisa's wrist with her fist until Lisa's hand gave way. The streaking pain in her hand shot up her arm like jagged lightning. Lisa thought her arm would fall off from pain and she was sure her ankle was broken. The agony was excruciating.

"Mama, stop. Please stop. I can't go any farther," Lisa moaned.

"You can and you will. We only have a little further to go," Millie stated firmly.

"Why, Mama? Why are you doing this? What have I ever done to deserve this?" Lisa asked woefully.

"You know the reason, Bethelee," Millie mumbled and looked away from her.

"Bethelee? No! I'm Lisa, Mama, not Aunt Bethelee," Lisa said in alarm. "Mama! Look at me. I'm not Bethelee. I'm Lisa; your daughter."

Millie looked at Lisa and snarled. "I know who you are. Always thought you were better than everybody. Thought you would go off and become a *big* singing star and just leave the rest of us. Well, you ain't gonna be no big star and you ain't gonna give us no illegit brats!"

"Mama, it's me, Lisa. Please. See me, Mama. Me!" Lisa cried out. Millie was caught in a hellish vortex of the past. She had done something real bad to Aunt Bethelee and she was reliving it. Millie was totally con-fused and intent on doing something very dangerous and cruel. But it wasn't Aunt Bethelee that was caught in her evil grasp—it was herself and she had to talk her mama around. Her only chance was to bring Millie back into the present. She had to get through to her.

"Get up," Millie snapped.

"I can't! Mama, look at *me*. Talk to *me*. Tell me why you're so angry with me," Lisa pleaded.

Millie squinted and then rubbed her eyes. She cocked her head to the side and stared at Lisa in puzzlement. Lisa gazed into Millie's cloudy gray eyes; willing her to recognize her.

"Let her go, Millie,"

Millie swung around and saw a shadowy figure in the distance. She leaned forward and peered into the thickening fog.

"Who's there?" Millie demanded.

Lisa followed Millie's gaze but could see no one.

"Who's there, I said. Answer me," Millie shouted.

Strangling fear rose in Lisa's throat. She thought she was going to choke on it as she put a hand to her throat.

"Mama, no one's there. Who are you talking to?" Lisa whimpered.

"Shut up, Bethelee. It's probably one of your young studs come to get you. But he can't have you—not until I'm done with you," Millie carped.

Lisa thought that she had witnessed a glimmer of clarity come over her mother. But it had quickly vanished into the fog.

"Mama, listen to me," Lisa wailed.

Millie turned and swiftly kicked Lisa. Lisa screamed in pained, clutching her hip.

"Stop, Millie. Let her go,"

The dark figure moved forward. Millie gasped.

"You stop right there. Stay where you are. Don't you come near me," Millie shouted.

Lisa thought Millie had completely lost her mind. No one was out there.

"Leave her be, Millie. You got to stop."

"Stay out of this. Ain't no concern of yours," Millie replied with distain.

"I won't let you harm the girl."

Millie laughed wildly. "And what do you think you can do about it? You're dead!"

Lisa thought she would pass out. She was scared out of her mind. Was Mama really talking to a ghost? And if so, who was it? Millie was laughing uncontrollably. In her mirth, she had walked toward the apparition, leaving Lisa a good distance behind her. Lisa began to slowly push herself backward.

"You're dead, Leon. There ain't a thing you can do to me—not anymore. You can't beat me for not having dinner ready on time. You can't berate me for wearing old clothes. You'd conveniently forget that you wouldn't let me buy new ones. You can't slap me because the baby cried. You can't humiliate and disrespect me by whoring with your sluts anymore. I took care of that. Didn't I? I made sure you wouldn't shame me ever again, didn't I?" Millie sneered.

Lisa clasped her hand over her mouth. She didn't want to believe what she was hearing.

"Maybe in your mixed-up mind you had good reason for what you did to me. Maybe I deserve it for how

I treated you. But you've got no reason to hurt Lisa," Leon said.

"Let her go, Mama,"

Millie looked sharply to her left. "And what do you think you're going to do, Rob? Save the day. Getting rid of you was the best thing I've ever done for Josie. You didn't love her, not like you should have. She was as high over you as ice cream over poop. You should have been groveling at her feet to show how much you loved her. Instead, you were busy grabbing your pleasure from any whore who would have you. You were more concerned about satisfying that stick between your thighs than taking care of Josie and the children. I should have done it long ago. Cutting you down was as easy as throwing out the trash. You never saw it coming, dumbass!"

"I never cheated on Josie," Rob said as he moved forward.

"Josie may have thought you were telling the truth when you said you was going out with the boys, but I knew better," Millie yelled.

"You're wrong, Mama. I loved Josie with my life. I never would have dishonored her that way," Rob replied.

"Liar! You did cheat on Josie, but you won't anymore. You're dead and it was the best thing I've ever done," Millie roared. She swung around with her arms outstretched to face the phantoms. "So, what ya'll gonna do now? You know you can't stop me. Hell! I'm the one who stopped you. You gonna call out Richard and Patrick?" Millie shrieked hysterically. "Do they have a bone to pick with me too?"

Tears were streaming down Lisa's face as she continued to scoot backward away from Millie. Suddenly, she felt an arm wrap around her. She opened her mouth to scream just as a hand clamped over her lips.

"It's all right, Lisa," a heavy Scottish brogue whispered. "I've got you."

Lisa collapsed against Duncan in exhausted relief. He quickly cradled her in his arms and moved silently away. Millie, absorbed in her demented rage, had not noticed them. Duncan reached the shocked assembled party and deposited Lisa to her loved ones. The girls quickly comforted their sister. Duncan motioned with his head for the men to follow him. They crept back to the clearing where Millie was crowing about her triumphs. Standing behind thick trees, they were well hidden from sight. They covertly watched her.

"Well? How are you gonna stop me, Leon? Rob? You can't," Millie said scathingly. "You were good for nothing when you were alive and you're worth nothing dead."

Two more figures joined the phantoms.

"So the two of you decided to join the party? So nice to see the both of you but you're dead too. Thanks to my handiwork. I'll do anything to protect my girls. And you two had to go," Millie said harshly.

Richard and Patrick's ghost slowly advanced toward Millie.

"You'll be able to do about as much as Leon and Rob. Nothing," Millie laughed. She looked behind her and realized Lisa was gone.

"Where is she? What have you done with her?" Millie demanded to the specters. "Give her back to me."

The ghosts stood in a horizontal line facing her. They were resolute in their bearing.

"It's over, Millie. I know I treated you wrong but you had no right to take it out on our daughters' husbands," Leon said.

Suddenly, everyone could hear and see them. The apparitions literally materialized out of the bitter-cold air. The sisters gasped, clasping their hands over their mouths as they watched from afar. The men looked at each other in awe then quickly turned their attention back to Millie and the ghosts.

"You've done enough, Mama. You've murdered every spirit here. The killing stops now," Rob inflexibly.

"Rob!" Josie called out.

Millie turned at the sound of Josie's voice.

"He can't help you now. He never could. That's why I killed him," Millie shouted as she looked at her daughters. She pulled the sinister-looking needle from her pocket and pointed it toward Rob.

"Rob," Josie cried as she took a step toward him.

"Stay back, Josie," Rob warned.

"Listen to your dead husband, Josie. For once, he's telling you the right thing," Millie sneered.

Millie saw Lisa sitting on the ground, propped against a tree near her sisters. Millie took a step toward her. Angie stepped in front of Lisa as Josie, and Sandra knelt on either side of her. Sam stepped forward and drew his gun.

"Stop, Millie. Let's end this now," Sam said.

Millie laughed hysterically. "You can't stop me. I'm doing what's right, what grandma would want me to do," Millie screamed.

"Don't come any closer, Millie," Sam said. "I won't let you harm her."

"Get out of my way," Millie hissed as she slowly inched toward them.

Millie continued to move forward but was halted as the four ghosts suddenly appeared several yards in front of her.

"Nooooo," Millie screamed. "You won't stop me. Grandma told me, it's for the best."

Millie began running toward Lisa, waving the needle wildly. The men began chasing after Millie. Millie ran as if demons were on her heels. The ghost slowly drifted toward Millie. It seemed to Josie that they weren't really walking but oddly floating. She couldn't see their feet, just the empty bottom of their pants swaying in the wind. The eeriness of it intensified her fear. She hugged Lisa tightly.

A guttural sound erupted from Millie's throat as she charged toward the Lisa, the heinous needle raised in attack mode. But she didn't see the protruding tree root bulging through the earth. She tripped awkwardly over the root and flew toward the ground. During her downward flight, she brought her arms forward to break her fall. In doing so, the needle twisted inward to her body as she landed on the cold, unyielding terrain emitting a horrific groan. The men reached her side and Derek rolled Millie onto her back. The ground had driven the needle completely into her chest. But it wasn't the needle protruding from her chest. It was a dagger. No one understood what had just happened. Derek would have sworn it was the same knife that was locked in his desk drawer at the station. But it couldn't be, could it?

"Mama," Sandra cried out as she and Josie raced to Millie's side. Angie assisted Lisa as she hobbled to their mother's prone body.

Duncan felt the side of Millie's neck for a pulse. He looked at Josie and sadly shook his head negatively. Everyone was stunned to see a hook-handled knife jutting from Millie's body instead of the needle. They looked at each other in shocked bafflement.

"It was the needle that was in her hand," Josie said near hysteria. "I saw a needle."

Duncan held Josie close to him.

"I saw it too," Angie wailed. "She had the needle."

"This is impossible," Sandra wailed. "She can't be dead from a needle."

"But it's a knife in her belly," Lisa said. "How?"

They all silently stared at each other. No one had an answer.

"It is done," Leon said quietly.

Everyone turned to look at the specters as they began to slowly disappear. Rob smiled at Josie and blew her a kiss as he vanished forever.

Tears streamed down Josie's face.

"It'll be all right, Josie. All will be well," Duncan whispered.

The sisters knelt at Millie's lifeless body and cried. Millie was dead.

EPILOGUE

Josie gently swayed on the porch swing and watched the birds soar in the sky. It had been eight months since she and her sisters had laid their mother to rest. Josie still remembered that day as though it had only occurred just yesterday. Everyone had spoken about Millie and the ghosts extensively. It had been hard to take in the significance of what they had learned. They had watched their mother turn into a deranged person that they no longer knew or understood. Millie had harbored a lot of resentment, anger, and misplaced loyalty due to Leon and their great grandmother. It had turned her into a troubled individual who eventually could not distinguish reality from delusion. Her past became her present and she began to relive that life to avenge her husband and please her grandmother, both of whom were long gone. It was her children who had to bear the brunt of her tormented anger. But they had survived and had moved on. Millie was now a part of their past and could no longer hurt them.

Josie no longer felt the sorrow that had consumed her on that dark, rain-dreary day. She had dealt with the pain and put everything in a plausible perspective. She even received a message from Rob in a dream. He had explained his earlier cryptic message to her. She now understood that she had spoken too much to Millie about her relationship with Rob. Although Mama was now gone, she vowed never to make that same mistake again. She would discuss any problem she may have in her relationship with Duncan to him only. Josie smiled. It felt good to be in a relationship with Duncan. They had grown close and he had been her rock when she'd needed him most. Life had continued on since Mama's death and so had her family. In fact, life was safer, happier, and more peaceful for everyone. Answers had been found to burning questions and closure had finally been given, allowing the past to be a memory and the future to be joyfully anticipated. Her sisters were enjoying the present with a light heart and ready smiles on their faces. Angie and Derek were expecting their first child and the couple couldn't be happier. They didn't know the sex of the child, so Josie was cheerfully buying colors befitting a girl and a boy. Angie told her she was spoiling the child before he or she arrived, but Josie laughed and said that was her job as a doting aunt. Sandra's diner was thriving and she was gleefully counting her bounty and planning the café's expansion. Jimmy had finally opened his private practice and had more clients than he could handle. He'd hired a young lawyer who had recently passed the bar to mentor and share the workload. And Lisa landed a record contract due to a contact that Duncan had in the music industry. She recorded her first hit and was over the moon with joy. She's sharing her happiness with Sam whom she'd been dating since Mama's death. Wedding bells were expected in the near future. Duncan seemed to ingratiate himself into the family with ease. He was humorous, courageous, loyal, and hardworking. And it was obvious to all with functioning eyes that he was madly in love with Josie. Duncan's past was somewhat dubious at best but Josie didn't pry. Quite frankly, she really didn't care. He was from a different world and the traditions, standards, and culture of that society led Duncan on a diverse and oftentimes radical path. But Josie was accepting of his current life and did not worry about his past. He admitted that he had done some things in Scotland that were somewhat less than ethical but swore that he had done nothing that would come back to haunt him or harm her or her family. And Josie believed him. She trusted him and knew that she could count on him. Duncan had a knack for designing and constructing, so it was a no-brainer that he would study architecture. It had blown her away when she discovered that Duncan had a bachelor's degree from the University of Scotland. He was a man of many diversities and accomplishments. He was always surprising her with new facets of his character. Life with Duncan was never boring. She looked forward to becoming his wife. Knowing he would always be with her, no matter what, made her delirious with joy. Oh, how she loved him. Josie smiled brilliantly as she saw Duncan turn the corner and jog to her house. He bounded up the porch steps and sat next to her on the glider. He cupped her face and tenderly kissed her lips. She reveled in the caress. He gave her a final peck then sat back and pulled her against him.

"How was your day, darling?" Duncan asked.

"It was lovely. Kimberly was superb in ballet class and little Robbie has been the epitome of a perfect baby," she grinned.

"The epitome?" he questioned.

"Yes, Mr. McKinney, the epitome," she happily responded.

Duncan smiled. Josie enjoyed saying his last name ever since he had told her what it was. It was her way of telling him that he was no longer a loner living a questionable, dubious life. He was now a major part of her life, and would always be.

"Hmm, let's just hope he remains so for the rest of the evening," Duncan retorted. "I want to show you just how much I love you."

Josie laughed. She loved their light-hearted banter. They were as relaxed with one another as an old, married couple. They could discuss anything, good or bad, with a touch of humor. It made the good better and gave the bad stuff a brighter outlook.

"Duncan, tell me about your childhood," Josie whispered. She'd wanted to ask him about it on several occasions but had been afraid to broach the subject. She wasn't sure how he would react. But he seemed so comfortable and peaceful now. Maybe he would open up to her.

He didn't say anything for several moments. Then he took a deep breath, expelling the air slowly. "My childhood was not a carefree life, especially in my early years," he said softly. His brogue was deep and distinctive. "Life was hard. I never knew my father and my mother gave me little to no attention as she was always sorely tired from scrubbing houses all day and washing other people's clothes all night. I remember that she was so thin and fragile. Although she was frail and faint from her drudgery, she never stopped working. One day, I begged her not to go to work. She was having chest pains and was weak from lack of food. But she said she had to go work. She couldn't afford not to be paid for a day. Trying to feed and clothe six kids on fifteen dollars a week was a constant worry for her. When she got home that night, she collapsed into an old wooden rocker, totally exhausted. I sat on the dirt floor beside her, worried that she looked so tired and pale. She held my hand tight and apologized for not doing better by us bairns. I told her she was doing fine. We all would be fine. But she shook her head and gave a weak smile. Suddenly, she had a wretched pain. She doubled over clutching at her chest. I held her close, willing her to be all right. She died in my arms. It was probably a heart attack that took her away. The hard life with no help had taken its toll on her. She was too young to die but too drained to go on living. I was nine years old when she died and from that day forward I had to be a man. I was living on the streets, rummaging through garbage for whatever I could use to help me stay alive. I stole, begged, and did nefarious jobs for scraps of food. I would do almost anything to survive. I've done some things that I am not proud of but staying alive for another day was my only concern."

"I'm so sorry," Josie murmured.

He squeezed her shoulder and kissed the top of her head. "In a way, I am grateful for those hard years, for they shaped me into the man that I am today. Those early years taught me to be strong, courageous, and tenacious. To recognize what I want and not be afraid to pursue it," he said quietly.

"You're a wonderful man, Duncan. You've been through so much yet you not only survived but persevered and achieved," Josie responded passionately.

"I had help. Help from a loving couple that saw something in me that they wanted to nurture and cultivate. As an adolescent, I roamed the fields and streets of Glasgow, pandering and bartering for a meager survival. One cold, bitter night, I found shelter in a run-down barn. Lying on a dirty bale of hay, I fell asleep only to be abruptly awakened by an elderly farmer. The kindly farmer took pity on my situation and invited me to the kitchen for warm bread, cheese, and a mug of milk. The farmer's wife insisted that I needed rest so she tucked me into a clean, soft bed. It was the best sleep I had had in years. I slept so peacefully. The next morning, I woke and began to make my way down the road but the farmer followed me and asked if I would like to stay with them. I could earn my keep by helping him on the farm. Not one to turn down a good offer when I saw one, I immediately said yes. They seemed to like me and we all got along well. I was always laughing and talking of having a better life when I grew up. They doted on me and lavished me with love. I came to think of them as my adoptive parents. I flourished under their care and love and I appreciated all that they did for me. I did all I could to help them. It wasn't long before they recognized my aptitude for construction. After building a farmhouse that could pass for a palace, they decided to send me back to school. I thrived in school and went on to college. But upon finishing, I still did not know what I wanted to pursue. So I led the life of a loner and embraced the role of an old world highwayman, taking advantage of opportunities as they presented themselves," he said.

"I wondered about that getup. You appeared very intimidating," Josie remarked.

"It was one of my quirks. It was amusing to see the look on people's faces when they encountered me. It also kept the outsiders at bay. I didn't want to let anyone know the real me," he said quietly. "It was one of my defense mechanism, courtesy of that kid on the streets that didn't trust anyone. The suspicion and cynicism remained with me for a very long time."

"I understand why you felt the need to protect yourself," Josie said gently.

"Old habits resist dying," he said somberly. "But I became very adept at capitalizing on excellent business ventures. I was able to provide for my adoptive parents. They lived in luxury for the rest of their lives. I also sent money back to my siblings. It was an exceptional opportunity that landed me in Brooklyn, New York, as an independent financier, and it's how I met Rob," he explained.

"When you loaned him the money," Josie stated.

"Yes. And you know the rest of the story," he sighed.

"I know that you protected my family and for that we will be eternally grateful," she said as she raised her head to kiss his cheek. "I know that you are now attending Pratt Institute for Architecture and will soon have your degree and certification to be an architect. And I know that you will open your own firm and build beautiful, uniquely sculptured buildings. Because you always achieve whatever you set out to do."

"Do I?" he smiled.

"You do. Which is only one of the reasons why I love you so much," she answered.

And she did love him. More than she ever thought possible. And she couldn't wait to become his wife in two months. There were so many things about him that she admired. He was thoughtful, caring, and loving, not only to her but to her children and her family as well. Her sisters loved him and thought Josie was the luckiest woman alive. She was so proud of him that she thought she would burst. She realized she loved him the night he had saved Lisa from Mama. He had spent the night, determined to keep Lisa and her safe. She had lain awake watching him sleep in that too small, uncomfortable chair and knew at that moment that he was special. He hadn't complained. Rather, he had kept a silent vigil on her and Lisa the entire night. It was then that she knew inexplicably that she loved him. She may have only known him for a short time but it didn't matter. In her heart, she knew that he was the man with whom she wanted to spend the rest of her life.

"You indicated that there are other reasons why you love me. What are they?" Duncan questioned slyly.

"Never mind. I'll not tell you. Your head is big enough," she laughed.

"Ahh! What does a man have to do to receive the smallest of compliments?" he joked.

"Well, you can tell me that you love me," she said impishly.

"I love you. I adore you. You are my every heartbeat," he said earnestly.

"And you can pick up where you left off a few moments ago," she invited.

"Will that get me another compliment?" he asked as he began lowering his mouth to hers.

"Oh, undoubtedly it will," she sighed as she looked into his burning, amber eyes.

"Never say that I'm not a man who aims to please," he whispered as his mouth covered hers.

It was a good thing that little Robbie slept peacefully throughout the night.

ABOUT THE AUTHOR

Melinda Avent has always had a passion for the written word. From an early age she was drawn to placing her ideas on paper. Her thoughts turned into plots and characters and stories were then born. Although interested in several genres of storytelling, she chose to focus on mystery for this book; which highlights elements of the supernatural. Born in Ohio, she currently resides in California where she continues to speak her heart through writing.

HD
nu

CPSIA information can be obtained at www.ICGtesting.com
Printed in the USA
LVOW10s0356140716

495511LV00010B/126/P